STEAL AWAY

RAYANNE SINCLAIR

Hopetoun Publishing
Edmonds, Washington

Rayanne Sinclair

STEAL AWAY
Rayanne Sinclair

HOPETOUN PUBLISHING
Edmonds, Washington

For more information about this book, visit
www.rayannesinclair.com

Print ISBN 978-0-9897502-0-2
Electronic ISBN 978-0-9897502-1-9

This is dedicated to the ones I love

Acknowledgements

This is my first book and the experience of publishing has been exhilarating. As a businesswoman I can't say that I've had a lifetime goal to write a novel, but it's now become a passion, so readers can expect more stories from me in the future!

One of the most gratifying aspects of this adventure has been the opportunity to work with a bevy of highly skilled women from the Pacific Northwest. These ladies have been instrumental in helping me develop, refine, and edit *Steal Away*. I want to appreciate them here and say thank you to my development editor, Nancy Wick; publishing consultant, Beth Jusino; cover artist, Jenn Reese; copy editor, Kyra Freestar; and proofing editor, Kathy Burge—lovely and brilliant women all.

Of course, I also want to thank my husband and family members for their support and advice along the way. Last, but certainly not least, I want to acknowledge my incredible beta reader and friend, Laura Vowles—a woman who never fails to tell me what I need to hear with just the right timing and care.

1

ANNE LEDWELL was home from college for good, a newly minted class of 1977 graduate of Penn State University. Her parents had traveled to collect her minimal belongings and take her home to New York City. The thought of having left home to achieve her degree but now being under her parents' roof again was anticlimactic, to say the least.

The twenty-two-year-old sighed heavily as she contemplated greeting her old bedroom again. As she hauled her luggage into the lobby to await the elevator in the New York apartment building, a somewhat audible whisper came over her lips—"What's to become of me?" She looked back quickly to see if her dad, heading into the building right behind her, had heard her muttering. Satisfied that he was busy juggling boxes of her belongings while speaking kindly to the doorman, she felt certain he hadn't heard her.

There was no need to make her generous and loving parents think she was ungrateful for all they had done for her. After all, had they not sacrificed for years to deliver up the opportunity for her to get an education? Kenneth and Ruth Ledwell had done this three times for three daughters now, Anne being the last. Her sisters, four and six years older, were both well into their careers. And her oldest sister, Clara, was married and already had two children. So, for Anne, coming home was a reminder of the tension between feeling dependent and wanting to make her own way in life.

With her long, flowing blonde hair and small frame of five feet and two inches, Anne still looked the child on the outside. However, there was a certainty about her manner that made her elders unsure whether to consider her fragile or strong. It was a bit of a mixed message to encounter such a petite young lady making declarative statements, as though she understood the world. The fact that she was beautiful and full of youthful optimism didn't make it any easier to take her seriously.

Sprawling across the white chenille bedspread she thought she had left behind, she stared at the bedroom ceiling and considered her last four years. Later she'd have to get to the dinner table and be sociable, but right now she just wanted to be alone. Thinking about her sorority sisters, the many things she had accomplished on campus, and the inevitable parting of ways that had taken place earlier this day made her melancholy. Did she miss everything and everyone back at school already?

Her thoughts then wandered to whether or not she should return to University Park—perhaps to graduate school or a job on campus. The reality immediately set in on that question, for Anne knew that things were never the same when you tried to return to a previous life. That realization came from a history of moving around the country and the world for most of her young life. Anne's dad was a retired military officer, and until recently the family had never had the same mailing address for more than three years. The fact that she had just spent four years in one location made that place seem more like home than anywhere else.

The football games, the friends, the leadership opportunities had all been so much fun. But the door back to Penn State was closed, and she knew it. She'd just have to parlay her experiences into something marketable in what she referred to as "the real world." Despite the busy last months of her senior year, she had interviewed with a few company reps on campus, but even a strong grade point average and all her activities hadn't landed her a job. Looking on the bright side, at least she'd already created her résumé. Anne knew she'd need to start sending it out right away. If she ever hoped to be independent, she would first need a steady income.

2

Two weeks had passed since Anne returned to live with her parents. Daily she asked herself how they could stand to live in the city, where she felt unsafe even mailing a letter in broad daylight. New York had mean streets in the 1970s. News of rapes, muggings, and murders on buses, on subways, and even just seven stories down from her bedroom was commonplace.

Venturing out of the building, beyond the protection of the sweet and burly African doorman, wasn't something she particularly enjoyed. However, each day her mother would attempt to get her out and about on those crowded streets. Frequently it was just to satisfy her mom's shopping habit. It was a habit of aimless wandering about the high-end department stores, with the endgame of eating lunch somewhere. Ruth Ledwell wasn't much of a fan of the crime-ridden city either, but she'd learned the rules: move quickly, act like you own the place, and don't flash cash around.

Though it had only been fourteen days, Anne wished she could be anywhere but in this seemingly endless loop of reading the classifieds and sending out her résumé. In fact, she thought, tomorrow she would ask her father if she could go to the office with him. Yes, that's the ticket—she'd walk to his building with him in the morning to get a glimpse of what productivity and hard work looked like again.

Anne's father was an exceptional man, full of wisdom and insight. Kenneth Ledwell was tall, lanky, and well-educated. He walked several blocks of the tough streets to work every morning—often the first to arrive at the office and the last to leave. That was his way and his work ethic. Kenneth had retired from the military eight years earlier and now was a corporate lawyer—chief legal counsel for his organization, in fact. But what always seemed more important to him was the fact that he had become an ordained minister later in life. He well knew the law, and he well knew scripture. The combination made Kenneth an excellent counselor. Why hadn't she seen this before? If ever there was a time to obtain excellent counsel, this was it.

The following Monday morning, Anne set out with her father to walk to his office. Given the two strides she had to take to keep up with his one long stride, she was a bit winded when they arrived in the expansive lobby of his building. He was probably walking faster today because Anne had made him late for all the fussing she had done to put her hair up on her head. Wouldn't that make her look older, more intelligent, and more sophisticated, she thought? No matter, she found it exhilarating to fly up the twelve stories on a smooth-riding elevator to her father's floor this morning. She also couldn't help but notice how shiny the floors looked after a weekend buffing by the custodial staff.

Ken introduced Anne around to some of his colleagues, ending up at the desk of his executive assistant. Linda was a buttoned-down and efficient woman in her late fifties. Every graying hair on her head was sprayed into place. She seemed to be more in control of the surroundings than her boss as she quickly handed off documents to Ken, noting which ones required his signature that morning.

Anne settled into the stiff couch outside her father's office with a book she had brought along. She had calculated which book to pull off her old bookshelf back in her room. She had selected one by American economist Milton Friedman—*Capitalism and Freedom.* Though it had been around a while, she thought it might reflect well to passersby that she had this tome in hand. She was, after all, a recent graduate of the dismal science.

Within the hour she could barely keep her eyes on the pages, which were running together. Shoving the book into her handbag, she poked her head into her dad's office to see if he might be in the mood for giving advice. Sure enough, he had some time for her prior to a meeting in his office in the next thirty minutes. Plopping down in one of his guest chairs, across from his desk, Anne thought she'd start by asking him if she should be casting her job search net even wider. Ken reminded her that the matter of housing was key to answering that question. He suggested that perhaps she should give her sister Victoria a call. Since Victoria was single and going to divinity school in Pennsylvania, she might be willing to share space until Anne could find work and pay some rent. There was also a cousin in Phoenix who could use a roommate, he mused aloud.

As they continued the discussion, Ken reminded Anne that the largest job markets would provide her with the greatest odds of finding work. Of course, she knew he was talking about big cities like New York, Los Angeles, and so on. She had to admit that free rent at home while she searched for a job was a good deal, but her internal restlessness for the next stage of life resisted that logic.

As the conversation turned to the type of work she'd like to pursue, a young man stopped by Ken's office, and her father eagerly waved to him to come meet Anne. She stood up to shake hands with the good-looking gentleman whom Ken introduced as a recent hire.

"James, I'd like you to meet my daughter Anne. She's just graduated from Penn State and is busy trying to land a job now," stated Ken.

James eagerly shook her hand and mentioned how relieved he was to have landed his job after several months of search. The sound of "several months" hit Anne like a ton of bricks, but she responded with an upbeat, "Congratulations!"

As the three were standing in the office, her dad's appointment showed up, so Anne quickly announced that she was going to go to the main lobby and would meet him there to make the trek home for lunch. However, James didn't seem eager to get back to his desk, so he walked with Anne to the elevator. To avoid awkward silence, Anne asked James about his job. On the way to the elevator, he told her he was a junior actuary in the pensions department. It sounded like a positively dreadful job to Anne, but she was glad that James seemed to find it exciting.

After saying her good-byes, the silky smooth elevator brought her back to the lobby downstairs. She spotted a masculine leather chair and parked herself there. Watching the people come and go passed the time for a while, but on a nearby table she spotted a travel magazine. Debating whether or not it was safe to leave her purse even for a few seconds to go pick up the magazine, she decided to take the risk.

Safely back in the chair, which was much larger than she was, she opened the pages to find a beautiful pictorial review of England, Ireland, Scotland, and Wales. As she leafed through the pages, stopping only occasionally to actually read the words, each photo became ever more engrossing. More than two hours had passed when Anne looked up to see her father standing in front of her inquiring of her readiness to depart for lunch at home. For a second she wondered if it might be wrong to shove the magazine into her purse before leaving, but she did it anyway.

The two continued their discussion of career choices on the way home, and once inside the apartment, they found lunch already on the table. It seemed that her mother had stayed close to home today. Ruth was a good cook, though she didn't really enjoy the craft. In fact, Anne's mother had lots of domestic talent but seemed to go out of her way to avoid using it.

Now in her fifties, Ruth was a beautiful woman—a fact that Ken often repeated to her. Having seen the old family photos of her parents as young adults, Anne could see why her father would have been attracted to the lovely blonde sweater girl he met on campus. The two had married when Ruth was just nineteen, so she never made it past her freshman year. Instead, she went to work as a secretary to support them during Ken's academy law school days. Occasionally Anne would even catch her using the ancient skill of shorthand when taking notes in church.

On this day, the three enjoyed a fine lunch as the conversation brushed lightly over several topics. As things came to a natural close, Anne decided to make a bold request of her parents. After laying the pinched magazine open on the table, she had made a pitch for the three of them to plan a vacation to the United Kingdom. Much to her surprise, they both embraced it with enthusiasm.

Despite moving and traveling all of her married life, her mother was almost more excited than Anne about the whole idea. Her father seemed game too and laid out the parameters of limiting the trip to ten days, but he also notified the ladies that he wouldn't be available for the trip until September.

It was now not even July.

3

THE hot, humid summer of New York City made it even more unbearable for Anne to endure purposeless shopping with her mother. She'd often beg off to stay home and continue her job search. Some dinnertime conversations pointed to possibilities of people her father knew who might be hiring, but nothing came of those leads.

It was on one of those dreaded shopping trips when Anne noticed a large, big-name brokerage house from the bus window. Convinced that she could make money in the stock market, she went home and prepared a cover letter on the old manual typewriter she had lugged home from college. Mailing it with her résumé, she thought good thoughts.

Within a week, Anne had received her response, though it was much like other responses she'd been getting. The brokerage house had no current openings for which she qualified, but they would keep the résumé on file for six months should something suitable arise.

The weeks had turned into months, but the excitement of her father returning with airline tickets one late August evening sparked imaginations all over again. Ken had also brought a map of the region, which the three pored over to make decisions about where to visit. Travel was second nature to the trio, so there would be few formal arrangements—just "the plan" that Father typically derived and held everyone to.

This trip would involve a flight from New York to London and three days of sightseeing in the city, followed by a short trip to the English countryside. Days five and six would involve the train to Scotland, for a quick visit in Glasgow; then they would finish up in Ireland before making their way back to London for departure. Ken made the trip plans around a visit with an old friend in Glasgow who was now pastoring a small church on the West End of that city.

For Anne, the photos in the magazine she'd hung onto seemed too beautiful for words. Now, however, she would soon be seeing the shires, the rolling hills, the crags, and the bustling cities. With a last name like Ledwell, she wondered if jolly old England would call to her this time. The family had visited that country ten years earlier, and though she remembered it fondly, she had to admit that it didn't seem like her ancestral home.

Anne was a third-generation American from Britain. Her maternal grandfather, who was born in England, had come to the States through British Columbia, where he had worked for the Hudson's Bay Company for several years. In fact, her mother's maiden name was so English that when in London years earlier, they had looked in the phone book only to find pages and pages of the surname. Even her father's side of the family was from England, though they'd been in America longer.

In preparation for the trip, Anne made a request of her mother to pick up some tea bags at the store next time she went. Anne had learned to drink coffee while working as a waitress part-time in a small coffee shop near campus, but for this trip she thought she might need to acquire a taste for tea.

4

FINALLY the day of departure had come for what had now been deemed Anne's graduation gift, despite the fact that her parents had already given her $500 on graduation day. She had carefully deposited the check in the bank but had since withdrawn $100 for the trip. September 19 would be a long, drawn-out process, traveling overnight across the Atlantic and arriving in London on the twentieth—a Tuesday. The threesome couldn't leave on the weekend due to Reverend Kenneth Ledwell having a preaching engagement in the city the Sunday beforehand. Doing pulpit supply wasn't unusual for him on Sundays.

Anne was beyond excited as they reached the John F. Kennedy International Airport that evening for a late-night flight. The plane would arrive the next day in the morning giving the family some recovery time before they hit the streets of London on Wednesday. The trick would be sleeping overnight in cramped quarters while one was completely wound up about getting to the destination.

As they checked bags and found seating at the gate, Anne pulled out the stolen magazine once again. With her mom looking over her shoulder to get another look at the lovely isles, it was easy to get lost in the pages again. The only thing that nagged Anne was the fact that she'd be returning to redouble her efforts to find work in the city. But she pushed those thoughts back, and before long the gate steward was making the boarding call.

As they settled into their three-seat configuration on the plane, Anne was grateful to her parents for giving her the window seat. Ruth was in the center, because Ken needed the legroom on the aisle. Last call and they were wheels up—winging their way to the United Kingdom. A kingdom, thought Anne—how enchanting was that? This time she decided she'd pay more attention to learning about the royals and their antics!

Ruth nudged her sleepy-headed daughter so she'd catch the morning sun of the next day on the horizon through the airplane window. Startled, Anne quickly recalled her excitement and pulled herself together. In this last ninety minutes of flight, the attendants were making one more round for coffee and tea. Of course, Anne requested tea, but this time requested "whitener" instead of cream. The British Airways flight attendant didn't bat an eyelash. She was a beautiful, tall, and stately brunette who told the family that she'd been with the airline since its creation just a few years earlier.

Anne asked her if she'd ever flown on the new Concorde plane that everyone was talking about. The attendant let on that she'd not even been inside one but confided that she hoped one day to be trained for the flight. The conversation caused Anne to wonder if she should apply to be a stewardess, but when she mentally tried on the idea, it just didn't fit. It wasn't travel and adventure that Anne longed for. In fact, it was just the opposite—a desire to settle down and be a part of something she could contribute to, much like she'd done in college.

With her shoes back on her feet, Anne listened intently to the pilot's light British accent telling the passengers that the temperature in London was currently 22 degrees. Despite having lived in Europe for several years, Anne hadn't really bothered to grasp the metric and Celsius thing. She pondered for a while, straining to recall the conversion, and finally realized that London was substantially cooler than the nearly 85-degree day she would have seen in New York. Regardless, the cooler weather sounded like a welcome relief to her.

Touchdown was fast approaching, and Anne was busy gathering her things to place in her purse under the seat in front of her. Her dad slipped her a stick of gum to help with ear pressure, which she gladly accepted. Soon the roar of the engines and the first bump of tires to ground were felt. As the plane taxied to the gate, there was much to see, as they had arrived in midafternoon. In fact, there would be plenty of time for gazing out the small window: their seats were so far to the rear that it would be a while before the family could disembark.

Once inside the terminal, Anne first noticed the smell—there's just something about the smell of Europe that is different from the smell of the States. She really couldn't put her finger on it. She thought perhaps it was that there seemed to be more smokers. But to her, the smell was literally earthier—like that of dirt after a rain. In any case, she was glad to be on solid ground, even if her parents were rushing her to customs and bag retrieval. She couldn't wait to be done with the tedious airport tasks and on to a cab ride to their London hotel.

Could there be anything much more exciting than coming around the corner to see a fountain square filled with Londoners bustling about? It was so much fun to see their fashion style . . . or lack thereof. The people were fascinating, to be sure, but the architecture of old was such a thing of beauty. Anne was almost sad to see the cab come to a stop at the front of the hotel. However, the next several days would be filled with sightseeing, riding the tube, and people watching.

5

ANNE couldn't exactly remember how her father came to know the Scottish pastor William McGinty. The dear man had been shepherding a small Presbyterian congregation in Glasgow for several years. It may have been his former military service that was their connection, as her father had been active in the Officers' Christian Fellowship. Perhaps the pastor had been part of the Officers' Christian Union for the UK military when their paths had crossed. In any case, it was where the family was headed now for a visit.

Since the trip started late on a Saturday night out of London, they would arrive early on Sunday morning. The excitement of having her own sleeper caused Anne to leave the dining car early for bed that night. Once in the cramped space, she quickly found her way under the covers for the night on wheels. Drifting off to sleep wouldn't be difficult tonight.

With father rapping on her door early in the morning, Anne knew she'd have to respond with force for him to hear her over the rail noise.

"I'm up—will meet you for tea shortly," she shouted.

Lifting the bed to the wall pocket, she had more room to try to make herself look presentable, even before making her way to the shared lavatory. Moving about in the small space, she did her dressing in Sunday clothes, fixed her long tresses, and put on as much makeup as was reasonable for church attendance. Gathering up her things to put into her overnight case, she made her way to the restroom prior to ultimately joining her parents in the dining car for a continental breakfast.

The train came to a slow stop in the station long after Anne had been gazing out the window at the big but dirty city of Glasgow. Soon the three of them were stepping onto the platform, when an older couple approached them in gleeful recognition. On the rail trip Anne had been reminded that it was at a conference at The Hayes in Swanwick of Derbyshire where the two men had first met. It was a conference to which Anne and her mother had accompanied Kenneth, when Anne was just twelve years old.

She had fond, but limited, recollection of that conference, yet she did recall a cute young English boy in attendance with his parents that summer. That young boy had asked her to walk with him along the pond near the main house one evening after dinner. She couldn't recall his name and even now was embarrassed recalling that the young boy had asked if he could kiss her. She'd never been kissed and wasn't about to be kissed on that evening walk. For a split second, she wondered why she had so abruptly turned him down. No matter, she thought, he was likely happily married now and living somewhere in England. Besides, she reasoned, she had always been sure of herself and must have had a very good reason for the "no kissing" rule at the time.

The McGintys were a lovely couple who seemed so full of life and joy. They greeted Anne as though she must remember them, though she honestly didn't. They had parked not far from the large and busy station, and they promptly guided the family to the car. The church service was to start soon, and Pastor McGinty needed his prep time, so they were quickly whisked away to the small but lovely "kirk" in a distant neighborhood of the city.

Squarely seated in what may have been the guest of honor pew (or more likely where Mrs. McGinty regularly perched every Sunday morning), the family settled in for the beautiful order of a traditional Presbyterian service. Though Anne's parents were Baptists, she had always appreciated the Reformed tradition and fully intended to take up residency in a Presbyterian church when she was finally on her own. Yes, there would be some theological differences between her and her parents, but in such things there was liberty in order to keep peace in the family. After all, Anne's sister Victoria was studying to become an ordained Lutheran pastor. And if her parents could tolerate that, Anne assumed there'd be no problem with her chosen house of worship.

That is, when she had more control over her own choices and wasn't living under their roof and abiding by their schedule.

Anne was having that creeping feeling again of what awaited her back in New York—the job search, her restrictive bedroom, and the constraints of living in a city she didn't like much. But with the jolting first note from the church organ, Anne snapped back into the present.

There was Pastor McGinty, entering up the center aisle with others, to take their places in high-backed seats at the front of the church. The strong notes of "O God Our Help in Ages Past" pealed out from the organ for the processional, which all rose to sing. The choir entered next in their black robes to take their places in the small loft on the platform. Not exactly Westminster Abbey, but the small congregation belted out "A thousand ages in Thy sight are like an evening gone." It all seemed quaint but reverent to Anne, and she was so ready to worship before God and with these people!

As the service proceeded through the prayers of the people, the sermon, and the offertory, everything seemed to be so right and in its place. But there was a final song to be had from the choir . . . or so Anne thought. The pastor announced that the last song would be sung by one of the parishioners.

From the right rear of the church strode a tall man who picked up a guitar from behind the piano up front as the organist was making her move over to the piano bench. As the piano introduction started, it was met by a full-throttle, deep baritone voice, and it took a few seconds for Anne to realize the song was being sung in the old Scottish language. She surmised that it must be a hymn of some sort, but not a tune she had ever heard before. The gentleman's beautiful and forceful tones reached her very soul, and she was carried away as the choir joined with his voice in the last refrain.

Upon the benediction, the Ledwells weren't altogether sure what they should do as guests of the pastor. Anne's father indicated that they should probably stay seated and wait on their hosts, as the pastor would need to greet everyone at the church door upon exit. It was not difficult for Anne to stay seated in the little church and let the beauty of the service come back to mind. But that plan was interrupted a bit with very chatty and hospitable people coming by to shake hands and welcome them as friends of their "parson." However, within twenty minutes or so, the little sanctuary was empty, and the McGintys had reemerged from the narthex area to discuss meal plans. Anne's father had insisted that the McGintys join the family for lunch at any favorite place of their choosing.

For a moment Anne wondered if the couple ever really ate out, for these were not wealthy people, and this was not a town of wealth. But it didn't take long for Bill McGinty to lead the family back down the aisle and out to the sidewalk, while simultaneously carrying on about the haggis at nearby McLeod's Pub.

Anne smiled inside as she overheard him suggest that the pub was within walking distance. She was imagining her mother's internal double nightmare—walking any distance in heels, followed by walking into a pub! With a furtive glance at her mom, Anne was rushing to catch up with the two men and left the women several steps behind. This should be interesting, she thought. However, she was left wondering, what the heck was haggis? Oh well, she was game to try anything on this little graduation gift vacation of hers!

6

UPON arriving at the pub, the five settled into a high-backed booth that fit three on each side. Anne's parents let the other couple take the lead on what to order when the barmaid came around. Of course, she knew her Baptist parents were not likely to order what it seemed everyone in the room was drinking—Scotch or beer.

For a split second she thought about blurting out her own order of "I'll have what he's having!"–if it weren't for the fact that she hated the taste of Scotch and beer. It just seemed like it might be a fun thing to do just to catch the parental reaction. No, this would be a bit dicier than the playful Anne had thought—especially since she hadn't yet asked about the haggis. About halfway into the meals that they all finally settled upon, she did ask. Pastor McGinty was as delicate as he could be in his description, but midway through his explanation of its preparation, she wished she'd never asked.

Ken and the pastor were having a wonderful time getting reacquainted, and Anne noticed that the wives were also warming up to each other. The two couples seemed worlds apart to her—both literally and figuratively. And yet, the common bond of their faith had brought them together over this meal.

As she watched the four having great conversation, she felt that awkward twinge of being quite the useless fifth wheel in the whole equation. The feeling passed, however, when she reminded herself that they were just on vacation and would likely never see these people again. As her mind was drifting, she searched the pub to observe people in their everyday life. She wondered what it must be like for them, and whether or not they were really such fast friends as they seemed to be . . . or was it just the alcohol making them friendly.

No sooner had she found herself staring off into what looked like a backroom of the pub, Anne sat up straight and went stiff. There was that long-striding man who had risen to sing in church, heading toward their table. Before the others were even aware of his presence, he plopped himself down across from her and slid into the remaining space on the booth bench next to the McGinty couple. Acting extremely familiar with them—almost like a son or other close family member would do—he put his arm around Mrs. McGinty and gave her a hug.

Every eye was now upon the gentleman, while the pastor immediately and heartily greeted the man and started introducing him to the out-of-town guests.

"Why, Grant, you rascal—I want you ta meet ma friends from America! Ruth, Ken, and Anne, this is Grant Donaldson, who sang this mornin' in the service. Wasn't that a lovely Scottish hymn? Grant wrote it himself—an the congregation loves ta hear Grant sing anytime we can get him ta do so! That is, when he isn't tryin' ta make some extra money on the side with that melodious voice in joints like this one around town."

The chatty pastor hadn't even given the gentleman a chance to speak, but Grant was already shaking Ken Ledwell's hand across the table and greeting Mrs. Ledwell and Anne with his dancing hazel eyes. Once the pastor took a breath, Grant jumped into the conversation with his thick Scottish brogue: "I saw you in the kirk an wondered if we had new members! It's guid ta meet you."

No sooner did he get a word in edgewise than the good pastor picked up again with further explanation about how Grant's family had been members of the church for many years, and he was like a son to them. That certainly explained what seemed like an abundance of "overly familiar" behaviors to Anne, though she wondered if that was the "overly proper" British background in her reacting to the scene. Still, this Grant character was quite charming and wore like familiar slippers in this setting. The only bit of discomfort she felt as he sat across from her was that his eyes kept coming back to her, as though he wanted to ask her a question but couldn't seem to get it out.

Anne had to admit to herself that she wasn't sure what to make of Grant Donaldson. Perhaps it was her uncertainty about his age. Yes, that was it—just how old was he? She wondered to herself. That might give her a clue about how to react to him, or if she should react to him at all.

Adding to her confusion was the fact that he seemed so much more mature than she felt. For all her self-assuredness, Anne had led a fairly protected life. To be sure, she was intelligent, and her college experience had certainly opened her eyes to many of life's vain philosophies and social ills. But for it all, she was still quite naïve to the world she had seen much more of than most of her peers would see in a lifetime.

She studied Grant as he spoke to the McGintys and her parents with his unassuming, polite, and deep-voiced tones. With her ear not yet in tune with his accent, she missed some things he said—even while her parents seemed to catch them. Sizing him up, she concluded he was approximately six feet tall (she was not at all sure what that would be in meters, of course) and larger than her father. His shoulders were broad, and he appeared to her to be a man of some physical strength.

His face had some signs of what Anne considered to be aging—a few creases in the forehead, and laugh lines. Grant's appearance was what Anne thought a Scottish version of Yul Brynner might look like. And since he was bald (or at least shaved to bald), she thought he must be closer to her parents' age than her own age.

Yes, that was it—he must simply be one of those men who preferred the company of older mentors and wise friends. Anne had made her calculations and determined he was probably just a very friendly guy who wanted to make sure that friends of the McGintys were made to feel welcome in a strange land.

She began to relax and go with that assessment as she returned to actually listening to the conversation, only to hear her father asking Grant about his musical sideline. Grant gleefully responded that he was just a tinker by trade, but his passion was his music.

In that instant, Grant's eyes returned to Anne again with that question mark look. She could have sworn he'd just asked if she'd like to come hear him and his mates perform at a local pub tonight. What was that? Her mind was racing—had he just asked her out? Was this just more extension of hospitality? Was she about to respond to the question of whether or not she'd go out with an older man, a stranger—to a bar in a country to which she'd just arrived and would be leaving tomorrow morning? She was now recalculating.

Before Anne knew it, it seemed everyone at the lunch table was in agreement, and she was assured of a seven o'clock pickup at their hotel to hear Grant's group perform. She heard his assurances to her father that he'd have Anne back to the hotel after the gig—certainly not later than ten, for he now knew they were leaving early the next morning. Then Ken Ledwell upped the ante.

"I'm not worried, Grant. If the two of you decide to get a bite to eat afterward, that's fine too."

Anne had a date, but she wasn't even sure when—or if—she was the one who had answered Grant's question mark.

7

THE McGintys had said their good-byes when dropping the family off at their hotel that afternoon after lunch. The Ledwells checked in to their small room with a secondary parlor area, where a sleeper couch could accommodate Anne in the same room with her parents. Knowing her father's propensity to save on expenses, it was not a surprise to Anne that she wouldn't have her own space. She plopped down on the couch and promptly fell asleep. Sunday-afternoon napping was encouraged in the Ledwell household, and within an hour she awoke to her father's loud snoring in the main bedroom.

It was a jolting wake-up as it came with the realization that she was supposed to be going to a pub in a few hours . . . with a man she had just met. For a second she wondered why her father hadn't been more protective and expressed reservations at the suggestion. Shrugging her shoulders and sighing aloud, she chalked it up to another foreign adventure, and she was determined to learn more about her surroundings. Meanwhile, she'd take this free time to catch up on a book she'd brought with her for the trip.

After the three ventured out for a bite to eat, by 6:30 p.m. Anne was back in their hotel room changing into bell-bottom pants and her favorite sweater. She thought she'd at least be comfortable on this outing, and it wasn't as though she needed to impress anyone. After emerging from the bathroom ready to go downstairs to meet up with Grant, her mother expressed concern about her attire.

"Mom, you know I've never liked wearing dresses. And, besides, I'm only going to a bar."

Anne could tell that her mother was none too happy about that fact, which successfully distracted Ruth from the matter of what Anne was wearing.

As she grabbed her purse, her father inquired about how much local currency she was carrying, and was it enough to get a cab back to the hotel, if that became necessary. Great, Anne thought, now he voices concern about this plan? Yes, she had some money on her and would use it if required. With that, she grabbed the room key and was off to catch the elevator to the lobby.

One of her pet peeves was being late to anything, so Anne made sure she was arriving several minutes prior to the 7:00 p.m. departure time. She was pleasantly surprised to see Grant springing up from the seat he had taken in front of the lobby's large, unlit fireplace. He greeted her with the same affable style she had seen in him earlier.

"Guid evenin', lass. Your car awaits you! I'll be your tour guide tonight in the lovely city of Glasgow," said Grant.

"Thank you, I'm looking forward to it!" she responded with a smile.

With that, they were off to the street, where Grant had parked about a half block away. As they approached his vehicle, he began apologizing for his elderly blue Opel Kadett. Anne might have been underwhelmed except that cars didn't hold much fascination for her. She mentally speculated that all men seemed to associate some kind of personal projection about their vehicles. She dismissed his comment and instead complimented him on having a car at all, as such a thing was quite difficult to maintain where she lived.

Besides, she thought to herself, though she had a driver's license, she'd never actually owned a car. Right then and there, she reminded herself that having a car was definitely on her list . . . after getting a job.

During the drive Grant made small talk as they passed old buildings, pointing out a demolition here and a new enterprise there. The city streets seemed to have more buses than cars, and there were still plenty of people out and about on this Sunday evening. As they made their way onto Argyle Street, Anne thought she saw an unusual pavement pattern on the road, from whence she figured the name was derived. She thought about asking Grant, which came first, the street name or what looked like argyle-patterned paving stones. However, she let him point out what seemed important to him. No doubt this street was familiar enough to him that he no longer even noticed the pavers.

The car pulled up along a side street, where Grant parked. He then explained that they were about an hour early to the appointed time for his band to be on stage. Clearly feeling the need to help his charge feel more comfortable about what she was to encounter on this date, Grant went on to explain that he would introduce her to the owner and then find her a table where she would have a good view of the performance. When the show was over, he would retrieve Anne to introduce her to his bandmates backstage. With that explanation, he popped out of the car and dashed to open her car door for her. That seemed so old-fashioned in this day of women's lib that was busting out all over back in her country. Nonetheless, she thought it chivalrous of him.

Inside the gin joint simply named Mac's, Grant gently took Anne's elbow and moved her to the bar, where he introduced her to Mac himself. The proprietor looked to be in his sixties and even a bit frail, but that didn't stop him from quickly making his way from behind the bar to greet Anne. She extended her hand to shake his, but he promptly took it by the fingers and raised it to his lips. With that sweet gesture, he looked over at Grant and winked. The two men agreed to seat her at a small round table near the front, but close to the bar, from where Mac would "keep an eye" on Anne for Grant.

As Grant disappeared through what looked like a stage exit door, Mac put his hand on Anne's shoulder and asked, "Naw, missy, what can I get you ta drink?"

Not too sure of herself in this arena, Anne hoped she wouldn't insult the host by not ordering Scotch or beer. So, she asked if he had wine. The old man threw back his head and laughed. "No, Miss Anne, there be no wine here—an naught found in these parts anywhere!"

Certain that she must have stepped in it, she quickly retreated to requesting seltzer water, which he probably used for mixing drinks.

"Are you sure about that, lass?" he asked.

Yes, she was sure about the request, but not sure she would like it much.

Anne repeatedly shifted in her chair and slowly sipped the awful seltzer water while waiting for the music to get started. There were already people in the pub when she arrived, but the place was filling up quickly. By 7:45 p.m. there were no more tables, and people were standing. At least two young men had attempted to strike up a conversation with her, but like an angry goose, Mac had chased them away. Anne contemplated the potential that she might actually be making enemies in this friendly place. But before she knew it, Mac was on stage introducing the talent. It seemed that Grant was part of an all-male cast that played and sang familiar local music, and the growing crowd was eager to hear from them. The room was filled with smoke and the smell of booze and fried foods. Additionally, the temperature in the room was starting to make Anne wish she hadn't worn her favorite sweater.

Making an entry first was Grant, who introduced each one of his bandmates as they appeared individually on stage—Andrew, Conor, Ryan, and Ian. They made up a band called Clan Destin. The guys looked younger than Grant and were quite an attractive lot. As Anne looked each one of them over, she calculated that they were closer to her age, and so very cute. She wouldn't describe Grant in that way, for he was manly, while these boys were . . . well . . . boys.

In any case, those thoughts quickly passed as they each attached themselves to an instrument and began playing a Scottish reel that brought the house down. What talented musicians they were, thought Anne. She loved music—all kinds—and she was already tapping her feet under the table.

What must have been a rash of old favorites, seemed to roll over the locals in the establishment. With each number they clamored for more. Some tunes were raucous, while others were sweet, and still others were mournful. Anne noticed that many of the songs were about laborers, love, the land, and Scottish history.

Toward the end of a nearly sixty-minute set, Grant's guitar strummed an intro, and a beautiful harmony came from the stage. *"Why can't we just steal away, to a place unknown . . . "*

While the group was singing the refrain, the youngest of the band, Conor, walked down the few stage steps toward Anne. Holding out his hand for her, he walked her up to the stage and began singing the first verse of the song to her: *"Let's steal away—so far that no one will find us . . . "* Anne was embarrassed but endured the serenade as the crowd oohed and aahed.

Another repeat of the refrain was followed by Grant "cutting in" to stand between Conor and Anne, where he sang the second verse to her. *"We don't need much, leave it all behind . . . "* His warm and deep voice enveloped her, and it was as though he really was singing only to her. The verse ended, and breaking into her reverie, Conor took her by the hand again and walked her back to her table as the beautiful song concluded.

With that, the band members moved to the front of the stage and took a collective bow. The crowd pleaded for just one more song, and it appeared that the gentlemen on stage were going to oblige them. This last song started with hard guitar strumming and had a definite cadence to it. Apparently recognizing the number, the crowd began clapping and then hushed.

It was a song that Grant belted out with his strong voice, receiving only minor backup singing from the rest of his mates on stage. It was an earthy love song, and that was probably why he didn't make eye contact with her—never seeing her blush. But with the final words sung in drawn-out and softer tones, Grant turned toward her and stood squarely in her sights.

"So I'm left with only dreams of our time together . . . " As he sang, his hazel eyes locked onto hers in a way that precluded her looking away. For what was likely just seconds, but seemed like an eternity, she was bound up in his eyes.

8

LOOKING down at the empty glass before her, Anne realized she had finished all her seltzer water over the course of time, despising every sip. No matter—she was still reeling from what had just happened at the end of that last song. Was that a decision on his part, or just part of the stage presentation? Was it a realization on her part, or just a mistaken impression? One could hardly characterize it as an out-of-body experience, because she felt it deep in her body—at the core. But without any time to replay the interaction and connect the emotion with some rational thought, she chose to discount the entire thing. "Put it away," she whispered to herself.

Mac appeared as if from thin air to escort her backstage, where he said he needed to "deliver" her to Grant. As she made her way with him, Grant was already in the backstage hallway coming to meet them. He was jovial and seemed quite energized by all the hard work of performing. Situation normal, thought Anne—she was right to put it away.

Grant thanked Mac for his watchful eye and proceeded to direct Anne to a backstage room where he introduced "the lads" again—as though she hadn't caught their names when he'd announced them on stage. Each young man was courteous in his own playful way, yet they consistently glanced toward Grant as if to make certain they were being appropriate. They all seemed so deferential to Grant that Anne couldn't help but wonder if they saw him as a father figure, or perhaps an older brother. Anne praised them all roundly for their talent and thanked them for making her short visit to Scotland unforgettable.

Grant bid them all good-bye and gathered up his guitar. Holding out his crooked arm, it took a second for Anne to realize she was to latch onto her escort. As they made their way out the backstage exit, they spilled out into a dimly lit alley. Anne held tighter to Grant's arm, so much so that he took notice.

"Don't worry, lass, this is ma city—an I know it well. You're safe with me."

Approaching the car, Grant opened the trunk and gently placed his guitar inside. It seemed to be more than just a tool of the trade to him. Clearly this was a man who was passionate about making music. As she was contemplating that, she noticed a sense of urgency had come over him when they slipped into the car.

He hadn't started the car, but instead turned to Anne and asked—almost pleading—if she would let him take her to a small eatery several blocks up the street for some dinner. He acknowledged that it was getting close to the time he had told her father he'd bring her back to the hotel, but once again, it was as though there was a question behind the question.

Anne readily agreed to go. After all, she was hungry and even hungrier to learn more about Grant's question.

Driving along in silence, Anne felt obliged to fill the void. "Thank you for bringing me along to the pub tonight. The band is wonderful, and you have a very distinctive voice compared to the others. I really enjoyed the music."

Grant did not respond as he parked the car outside what looked like a small shop with an unusual name Anne couldn't pronounce. He jumped out quickly to open her door again on the street side. As they walked in to the café, Grant mentioned that the owners were an older Hungarian couple. He assured her that the food was simple but very good.

Seated at a square table, with very few other people in the place, Grant recommended the goulash. "I'll have that," she promptly responded. As a young waitress came by to take their order, Grant requested the same for both of them—the goulash and hot tea.

With that out of the way, he moved his chair closer to the table and leaned in across it. As large of a man as he was, this put him immediately and tightly in front of her face. This time she couldn't put it away. Those hazel eyes were looking deeply into hers, but with no words or stage act as accompaniment.

Finally, Grant reached out his hand to touch her hair. It was as though he was checking to see if she was real . . . or really there. Anne didn't move away, for she was again transfixed by his gaze. At last, he spoke what she wasn't prepared to hear or think about.

"I must see you agin, lass."

Shaking off the sinking feeling of reality, she smiled weakly and mustered a faint, "Well, perhaps you could swing by the hotel in the morning to say good-bye to us."

He quickly responded with continued seriousness and urgency, "You don't understand."

Oh yes, she understood alright. She understood that she was leaving in the morning with her parents for London, via Ireland, and then home to New York. As she slowly outlined that itinerary to him, the waitress brought their bowls, bread, and tea. It broke the tension as they gathered themselves for the meal. Grant took her small hand and quietly spoke a prayer for both of them in thanks for the food.

For the next hour, the two asked each other questions about their lives, interests, family, and more. They exchanged mailing addresses and phone numbers, and in the end Anne went out on a limb and informed Grant that she very much wanted to see him again too. With that, he seemed less agitated as he paid the bill, and they returned to the car.

All the way back to the hotel, the car was filled with chatter as Grant described his family of mother, father, and two sisters. It turned out he was a middle child, and as the only son, he worked alongside his father in the family business—that of watch and clock making and repair.

Anne told him about her two older sisters and how she'd just finished college and would be seeking work in the world of "high finance" in the Big Apple. He seemed genuinely interested in the United States, New York City, her family . . . but most of all, he pressed hard to know details about her. And she learned he was twenty-eight years old, clarifying in her mind how poor a judge of age she really was.

After parking near the hotel, Grant slow-walked Anne back into the lobby. Clearly not ready to say good-bye, he pressed the elevator button and boarded with her when it arrived. As the elevator doors closed, he pulled her close to him and gently kissed her.

As if startled by what he had just done, he put some space between them and said, "Hope I've not stolen from you that which I've no right to."

Remembering that boy she wouldn't allow to kiss her so many years earlier, this time Anne moved to close the gap between them again, and then quietly responded, "Steal away."

With that, Grant held her with his great strength and kissed her again, stopping only when the doors of the small elevator opened.

Walking down the hall to the room, Anne nervously retrieved the door key from her purse. Before saying good-bye and opening the door, she turned to Grant, who was already drawing her to himself again. As he clutched her in one arm, he ran his other hand through her long tresses and then held her by the nape of the neck. As he poured himself out to her with only his tender look, she began to more fully understand the phrase as well as the feeling of "parting in such sweet sorrow."

He lingered just long enough for one more kiss before stepping back and saying good night. Grant then turned to walk back down the hallway, and as he did, he uttered, "I'll be dreamin' of our time together." She heard him.

Having slipped in the door quietly, hoping her parents were asleep, she found her mother asleep but her father sitting upright and reading in bed. He took his reading glasses off his nose, put the book down, and whispered, "How did that go?" She flashed a smile of approval and whispered back that she'd tell them all about it over breakfast in the morning.

Waving good night, she locked herself in the bathroom to change into her pajamas. Alone now, she stared at herself in the mirror for nearly a minute. Somehow she looked different—yes, she even felt different. It took hours to fall asleep.

9

THE next morning the sunshine entered the small window at the foot of the sleeper couch. Had she overslept? That couldn't be the case, because her father would have called out the military time to bring her about. Not a peep this morning. Her parents were still in bed, so she made haste to take over the bathroom for a good shower and makeover.

By 9:00 a.m. the threesome were packed up and heading down to the lobby, off of which was a small dining room. It was unclear if the small café was part of the hotel, or just attached and run by another entrepreneur. The host escorted them to a table by the front window of the restaurant. The table was set with pretty lace linens and lovely china teacups and plates. As the three took their first sips of coffee and tea, their heads cleared enough to talk about the previous night. Anne described the music, the people, the band, the goulash, the city, and more.

Sensing that she had left something out, her father asked about her date. Anne felt a flash of red rising upon her cheeks at even the mention of Grant's name. She responded by indicating that Grant was both a gentleman and a gifted musician. That seemed to satisfy her parents, who didn't press her any further.

Just as the conversation came to a natural stop, the host who had seated them appeared at their table again. He asked if her name was Anne Ledwell, to which she responded in the affirmative. He then placed in front of her a single green rose corsage pinned to white tissue paper, indicating he was delivering it from a gentleman who had dropped it off for her.

She unfurled the paper to find a small handwritten note inside, with only these words: "Wear this while you're in Ireland, and think of me."

She quickly pulled back the lace curtains of the front window she was sitting next to, only to see a blue Opel pulling away from the front of the building.

"From Grant?" asked her mother.

"Yes," Anne responded, with a thinly veiled note of sadness in her voice. She promptly pinned the rose onto her fashionable camel hair jacket and placed the note with great care into her purse. Just then their breakfast arrived, which Anne picked over. She had arrived at the table hungry, but that was now replaced by that sinking feeling of a forever loss.

10

THE taxi pulled up to the airport of Glasgow, which was clearly under some kind of construction to expand. Anne was fidgeting with her handbag as the family was preparing to exit the cab. She wasn't sure why, but then remembered that the note in Grant's handwriting was in there. It felt like her last connection to him, because she knew the flower would fade before she even returned to London for their departure home. She resisted the temptation to find the note now. It would just have to wait until they were fastened into their seat belts on the plane to Cork.

The flight was brief, and as they touched down in Ireland, Anne couldn't help but think that the land looked rockier than that of Scotland or England. She wished she'd been able to see more of the country of Scotland, but this part of the trip was moving very quickly. She even overheard her parents discussing how they probably should have made this a two-week trip, but there just wasn't the opportunity for Anne's father to get away from work.

Anne was beginning to regain some excitement about the Ireland visit, even while still feeling a bit sorry for herself. The short flight had allowed her to "get real" with her inner thoughts on what had taken place in Scotland. She had determined she'd not write to Grant unless he first wrote to her. It was a thrilling encounter, but how could anything ever come of a relationship with three thousand miles of separation?

Anne glanced down at the rose on her jacket. He must have chosen the green rose as a nod to the Irish, in addition to it being a sweet gesture, she mused.

The family would be picked up by a tour guide in Ireland—one that they'd stick with for the two and a half days they'd be in the country before flying back to London. Arriving early enough in Cork City, the three joined with a number of tourists to enjoy an Irish lunch. They had already caught the influence of Saint Finbarr and would head to that cathedral after lunch. Anne was looking forward to seeing the architecture of Saint Anne's church and hearing its bells.

The busy day ended with tired feet from so much walking. As each tourist was boarding the bus for their accommodations up the road that evening, Anne was bringing up the rear due to her lingering. To be sure, she loved music and history, but it was the beauty of the buildings and their design that really drew her.

Approaching the bus, Anne saw her parents standing alongside the driver who was also their guide. Mick was a round and jolly fellow, most gifted with the "blarney" they claimed in Cork. As she came within earshot, he stopped Anne to ask her about her true love.

What true love? Her mind was racing—did she look like she was missing Grant? On the outside, that is?

"Um, I'm sure I don't know what you mean."

Mick pointed to the rose on her lapel.

"Oh, I received the flower as a gift this morning from a gentleman in Scotland. He told me to wear it . . . I assumed he meant 'the green,' while I was in Ireland."

Their middle-aged guide looked down at the ground and then back at her. Sheepishly, he inquired, "An that's all he told you?"

Anne was befuddled by his question . . . in fact, by the entire line of questioning. "Why, yes—I assumed it was perhaps a luck-of-the-Irish kind of thing," she replied.

The gentleman cleared his throat once and said, "Well, lassie, the wearin' of a green rose has a meanin' in this land. It tells all available lads that you're spoken for!"

Anne was completely conflicted by the revelation. She composed herself before the three of them standing there, and throwing her head back slightly, she responded, "No, he didn't tell me any such thing."

Her slight huff as she marched off to board the bus was a bit more noticeable than she realized, leaving the guide to remark to her father, "Hope I didn't do that young man in."

Removing the rose from her lapel in the hotel room that night, she was determined not to attempt to revive it in water overnight for a second day of wearing. She just kept wondering how Grant could have been so presumptuous. Or was he just toying with the emotions of a young American girl? Certainly, he must know that there was nothing but a single date and a few kisses between them. She stuck the pin through the heart of the rose and tossed the whole thing in the trash.

Alone in her room and with a husky voice, she mimicked Grant's words to herself in the mirror. "I must see you agin, lass." And in that instant the sting of tears came to her eyes. This time she raised her voice to the mirror. "You must have known we'd never see each other again. Why play me for the fool?" She threw herself on the bed and cried into the pillow lest anyone hear her.

The morning brought fresh perspective, probably due to a solid eight hours of sleep. And it was time for the tour to move on to Lismore, Waterford City, and then into Ireland's medieval city of Kilkenny. There was so much to see in this fair land, but in what seemed like the blink of an eye, the family was boarding a plane from Dublin to London. With just one more night in London town, the long haul back to New York was actually something Anne was ready for now. She pondered a future in a brokerage firm as she fell to sleep that last night in London.

11

THE flight home was uneventful, and Anne and her parents were getting back into their routine at home. During their first full week back in New York, Anne was delighted to receive a call from the brokerage firm she'd applied to earlier in the summer. They were calling to let her know that a support role had opened up, and they wanted her to come in the next day for an interview.

So on Tuesday of that week, she was dressed and ready to head out the door. Her mother wanted to accompany her to do some shopping while Anne was interviewing. As they boarded the cross town bus, Anne was excited about the prospect of perhaps landing her first "real job," even though she'd had temporary and part-time jobs in the past.

She rehearsed in her mind what they would ask her, and how she would answer those questions. Of course, her goal was to make a good impression, but mostly she wanted them to know she had a good work ethic. That thought brought her father to mind. He really was her hero when it came to such things. If he had ever not succeeded at something, she was unaware of it. She would hold him up as a role model in her mind throughout this interview.

Stepping off the bus, she parted ways with her mother, who had agreed to return to that exact same spot in less than an hour to meet her. As Anne walked the half block to the double set of glass doors on either side of the revolving door, she was in awe that any building would require so many doors!

Checking the watch she had borrowed from her mother, and realizing she had just five minutes to find the receptionist who would allow her entry to the interviewer Mr. Sevastian; she was already mentally rehearsing his name for her introduction.

Straight ahead and to the left past the elevators she marched. Building her confidence with each step, she even mustered up the courage to say "good morning" to a passerby in a dark-gray suit. He nodded but said not a word to her.

Finally she saw the receptionist at her desk, right in front of a massive piece of artwork that spelled out the name of the firm. It certainly was impressive, Anne thought.

Holding out her hand, she introduced herself and indicated she was here for an interview with Mr. Sevastian. Anne was so impressed when the receptionist stood up, shook her hand firmly, and stated her name. She then went on to ask Anne to have a seat in one of the chairs nearby, and she would signal to Mr. Sevastian that Anne was in the lobby waiting for him. Wow, Anne thought - someone who takes me, and her job, seriously. She took it as a sign of good training and good work standards. Now that's something she'd want to be a part of.

Within minutes a gentleman in his forties or so appeared and extended his hand to her, saying, "And you must be Anne Ledwell?" That was all she needed to reciprocate with confident business communications.

"Yes! Mr. Sevastian, I presume?" Firmly shaking her hand, he began chatting with Anne but then turned to thank the receptionist. Nice touch, thought Anne.

The two disappeared through double doors toward his office for the interview. The time flew by, and Anne was able to get most of her talking points across. Mr. Sevastian, who told her it was fine to call him by his first name of Nick, was both a good listener and a good interrogator.

After about an hour, Nick leaned in toward Anne over the desk and asked her how soon she could be available to start work. Was this an offer of work, she wondered ... or was he just checking in on availability? It took her by surprise, because he knew from their discussion and her résumé that she wasn't currently employed.

Despite her surprise, she promptly asked, "How 'bout tomorrow?"

He threw back his head and laughed heartily. Leaning forward in his chair, he reached out his hand to shake on it and said, "I'll walk you back to the reception area, which is exactly where I want you to report at 8:30 a.m. tomorrow to get started!"

12

OCTOBER 5 was an exhausting but exhilarating day for Anne. The first day on the job had been great, though it all seemed a jumble by the time she got off the bus that evening in front of the apartment building at 119th and Riverside. She was so glad to see the wide smile of Ben, their doorman, as he greeted her with "Howdy, Miss Anne! What say you about that first day on the job?"

She told Ben that she loved it as much as her feet hurt. He did his belly laugh and then called the elevator for her.

Once inside the apartment, she was half expecting both parents to be in the hallway asking her a million questions. Instead, she found only a note on the phone table: "Gone to dinner with friends across town—hope it went well today."

Just as well, she thought. This would be a good opportunity to make a sandwich and just watch some mindless television before hitting the sack early. After all, there were two more workdays before the weekend.

As she went to put the note back on the stand, she noticed an envelope with familiar handwriting and numerous foreign stamps and cancellation marks. She blinked to make sure she was actually seeing her name as addressee. How could this be . . . but who else would it be from, as it was clearly marked by a post in Scotland?

She kicked off her heels right there and ran into her room with the letter. Flopping down on the bed, she tore into the envelope with such vigor that one corner of the contents was ripped by the time she had the letter unfolded before her.

Before reading the words, she took in the entire page—looking first at the handwriting. After that, she picked it up and tried smelling it. All her senses were engaged as she finally began reading.

My Dearest Anne,

I am writing this letter the same night I returned you to the hotel. I can hardly believe that in a single day I met you and then I lost you. Thank you for agreeing to come to hear my band at Mac's this night. Thank you for lingering with me afterward at the restaurant. And thank you for allowing me to "steal" a few intimate moments with you before we parted.

I have already determined to leave a small gift at the hotel for you tomorrow morning, but won't interfere with your departure. Then I will post this letter so it may arrive to you soon after you are back in New York.

My mind is racing tonight, so I know I won't sleep well. My father will no doubt take notice of my weary self when I arrive at the shop tomorrow morning, but only after he gets on me for being past due to work! However, if he asks me if I had a date that kept me up late, I'll be able to answer affirmatively. I only wish I could relive that date over and over in real life—instead of simply in my mind. Truth be told, I'm not sure if I'll ever be able to get you out of my mind. I know this—I don't want to.

Anne, I was serious when I told you that I must see you again. Serious enough to make it my pledge to find a way to see you again before this year is out.

I also wish to know more about you. Tell me more—something—anything. If you will but return a letter to me, mine will not stop. Even if you don't write, they may not stop! Unless, of course, you do not feel the same way and wish me to cease the letters. That would crush me, but I will respect your wishes.

I trust the remainder of your holiday was good and that you are safely home with your parents. Please give them my regards.

Hold me in your heart, Anne—and know that you're in mine.

Grant Caelen Donaldson

Anne rolled over onto her back, holding the letter up in the air with both hands. She read it again, but this time she could hear Grant's thick accent in every word. She read it over again, and again—reveling in every word on the page.

"He was real," she whispered to herself. It had all seemed a dream since she saw him drive away that morning of their departure from Scotland. She felt a twinge of guilt for having tossed aside the green rose he had given her—and even guiltier for thinking him brazen. Clearly he was real, and so were his feelings for her. And though she was exhausted from her workday, Anne jumped off her four-poster bed and scurried over to her desk.

As she sat down, it was as though she had just realized how childlike the desk was. Her mother had purchased the small white desk for her room when she was much younger. Though she was physically about the same size now as she was at age sixteen, all of a sudden the desk felt like it no longer fit her. Yes, it was the right height, and she could write easily there, but sitting at the desk reminded her that she was no longer the teen who did her homework there and doodled on the heavy brown paper blotter that used to be there.

Anne pulled out some old stationery that was in the only and center drawer of the desk. It was a plain off-white color with an embossed gold A at the top and had matching envelopes. Not really caring what it looked like, she rummaged around for an available pen so that she might immediately respond to Grant's letter.

After nearly an hour of composing, thinking, and rethinking, she folded the letter and placed it in the envelope. She even sprayed the envelope with some of her favorite perfume. Addressing the letter, it dawned on her that this would not be something she could simply mail with the lick of a stamp and drop into the mailbox on the street below. This letter would require special handling at the post office.

Well, she thought, she'd need to figure out how that worked, because she was now determined to repeat the process many times over. For every letter Grant sent to her, she made a vow to herself to mail one to him as soon as possible.

Anne was awake in her bed when her parents arrived home from their dinner. Her light was off, and she pretended to be asleep, when out of her half-shut eyelids she noticed her mother open the bedroom door and quietly place Anne's shoes on the floor nearby. Since it was her parents who had left the letter under their note, she knew they must be curious about its contents. However, this night she just wanted to drift off to sleep and dream about that letter she had carefully tucked away in the Bible she kept on her nightstand.

13

A MID-OCTOBER frost was building a diamond-like sheen on the roads as Grant made his way home from the shop. He'd been working late on a couple of timepieces belonging to a local businessman so that they would be ready for him to collect the next day.

Grant felt particularly lonely that evening as he drove the dark streets to his small rented room above the elderly widow's kitchen. It was late enough—and cold enough—that he knew that Widow McBride would have already retreated to her bedroom. There'd be no light-hearted conversation with her over hot tea tonight in the kitchen they shared. Still, he was grateful to have a place to live at such a low cost. It was an unspoken bargain that he had with the widow, who had lost her husband to a fatal stroke twelve years earlier. Grant was both her renter and her protector.

His thoughts drifted back to an incident that no one knew about, except the two of them. It was a blustery and rainy night. Grant was attempting to write a song in his room with his guitar, when the widow answered the front door after hearing several demanding knocks and the voice of a neighbor from up the street.

It turned out to be old Kennedy, in a drunken stupor, who was trying to make his way home in the storm. The kind widow had let him in, but she promptly called out to Grant upstairs when Kennedy began groping at her. Grant appeared in a flash to defend the widow, pushed Kennedy back out into the storm, and walked him home. Grant had been soaked and chilled to the bone by the time he returned to a frightened but grateful Mrs. M.

Grant pulled his car up to the end of the driveway, closest to the back door entrance he used. Turning on the light in the kitchen as he entered the small house, he thought he might make himself some hot tea to take the chill off before bed. As he placed the teapot on the stove and reached for his favorite ceramic mug, he looked down at the counter to see a small, off-white envelope. He would typically pass over a mailing, assuming it was for Mrs. McBride, but he saw that it was addressed to him. Moreover, the envelope had a beautiful scent to it.

A wave of embarrassment came up as he considered that the widow would have noticed that lovely smell too—and that it had the return address of the beautiful honey-haired English-American girl he'd spoken to her about last month. Oh, only in passing had he mentioned Anne to Mrs. McBride—certainly not more than twice . . . or thrice.

Forgetting his intent to make tea, Grant pulled out the small pocketknife that hung on his keychain. He sat down at the rickety old kitchen table and carefully slit the envelope open. Before taking the letter out, he raised it to his cheek so he could take in the scent again. Now gently removing the letter, he began to read.

Dear Grant,

I sit at my desk just minutes after reading your letter—for the sixth or seventh time over. I've lost count. I can't begin to tell you how thrilled I was to receive it. To be honest, I wasn't at all sure you'd write. I never should have doubted your repeated promises to do so.

I'm not sure exactly what to say here in response to your request for more information about me, but since I know I have that same desire to know you, I'll do my best. My middle name is Elizabeth, and I am now 22 years old. I am 5'2" tall—which hardly qualifies as tall in any sense of that word. And, in this country it's considered impolite to ask a lady about her weight, but I'm not so vain as to be concerned to tell you that I weigh between 100 and 105 lbs. You'll have to translate those numbers into the metric system you grew up with, since I did not! Lastly, most American men are unduly interested in "measurements," but I am too modest to go into that and am not even certain you'd be interested. Suffice to say, I wear a size 5 shoe, dress, and everything else.

I have already told you a bit about my family, so let me tell you about what has taken place since I returned to New York. I recently landed a full-time job with a large brokerage firm in the city. In fact, I am writing this after my first day on the job. (Your letter, which I received upon my return from work today, was such a welcome gift.) I am working in support of a managing broker whose name is Nick Sevastian. My head is swimming in details that I haven't mastered from today, but I'm very optimistic about the position and can hardly wait to learn the trade, and to see my first paycheck.

It's now your turn to tell me more about you. Tell me about your job with your father. When did you start to work with him? How did you learn to do your job? How tall are you? You seem very tall to me—but then, everyone and everything seems tall to one as short as I am! Do you play sports of any kind, or is your free time largely taken up with your music? Do you play other instruments besides your guitar? When did you realize you had a passion for music? (And, an incredible voice with which to make music, I might add.) Should we attempt to exchange photographs?

Lastly, tell me more about your plans that we should see one another again. That seems like a dream to me, given the thousands of miles that exist between us now. But be assured that I think of you often—and the time we had together. Because of that, I do hold you in my heart—and hope we might see each other again.

I must try to get some sleep, which is going to be a challenge this night after reading your beautiful letter. No doubt I'll read it several more times before I put my head on my pillow.

Fondly,

Anne

P.S. Thank you for the beautiful rose you left for me at the hotel, which I did wear in Ireland. Someday you'll have to tell me what prompted that.

Grant leaned back in the creaky old ladder-back kitchen chair. Releasing a heavy sigh, he read the letter again ... and then again. The loneliness fled when he read it but overtook him again when he placed it back in the fragrant envelope.

He too had doubted, even once bethinking her the mythical Gaelic fairy lover—a *leannan sìdhe.* But this response to his letter made him feel that she was real, and maybe even within reach.

14

ANNE was curious as to why her parents never asked about the letter she'd received from Grant. She wondered if they were respecting her privacy; hoping the letter-writing campaign would simply burn out; or, perhaps, just feeling sorry for her.

It's not that she was moping around the apartment. No, she was focused on her new job and willingly helped around the place by cooking, cleaning, and occasionally going to the basement of the apartment building with her father to "watch" the laundry during that chore. But she was pretty sure they could sense that she would drift off when the three would pursue their board games in the evenings. In fact, her otherwise decent game of Scrabble was definitely off these days—leaving her father to win most of the time.

But there had been another matter that was adding to her distraction these days—one she hadn't told her parents about. Just three weeks into the job, Anne had met a gentleman at the office who invited her to join him for lunch down the street.

Joey seemed to fit the "tall, dark, and handsome" description very well, and he was a jovial sort who made Anne feel at ease in her new surroundings. Their first lunch together was something they'd planned out carefully, so as not to cause a stir of speculation in the office. They'd met just outside the lobby doors in the breezeway of the building. They even went their separate ways after hitting the reception area upon return.

When Joey and Anne sat in a back booth of the busy restaurant, no one even seemed to notice two young people in their early twenties chatting up a storm. The two actually turned out to have a number of things in common, with the exception of their ethnic background, as Joey was Italian. However, they'd both graduated from college that same year, so Anne got an earful of what campus life was like at an Ivy League school. Joey had received his business degree from Harvard. She was impressed with his credentials and his intelligence. She was even a bit envious of his status in the company, given that he'd been chosen for a fast-track management program already. It made her wonder if Nick might see her potential and recommend her for the program down the road.

Given the fun they'd had at their first lunch together, they promptly decided to escape again later that same week. This time it was Anne's turn to talk about her experiences at Penn State, where she'd received a leadership award in her senior year. That seemed to impress Joey, who had her recounting all the things she'd done there—serving as vice president of her sorority, taking part in student union leadership, and even chairing a major campus-wide annual event. As she recounted some of the other things she'd taken on, Joey was doubly surprised to find she'd worked part-time while attending school full-time during her last few years on campus.

"With all that going on, when did you find time to have a social life, Anne?" Joey inquired. Being an industrious and active person was just in her nature, so she thought his question seemed odd.

"That is a social life, isn't it?" she asked.

Joey laughed and then reached across the table, this time to take her hand, saying, "Well, that's not exactly the kind of social life I was talking about." She wasn't sure what to make of the hand-holding thing, but it certainly reinforced his meaning.

"I admit that doing all that along with trying to get good grades didn't leave much time for dating. However, that's the nice thing about being in the Greek system—the social activities are built-in. So, it wasn't as though I didn't have dates," explained Anne.

Joey seemed to be a natural at this, so it didn't surprise Anne when he boldly asked, "Yes, but did you ever date the same guy more than once?"

Anne fidgeted a bit in her seat and finally just blurted out, "No. And I wasn't sleeping around, if that's what you're getting at."

"Well, okay ... no need to get huffy. I was just wondering if there was someone special in your life," Joey stated as he removed his hand from hers to reach for his wallet. Diving for her own wallet, Anne apologized for being short with him. Being a good-natured sort, Joey didn't take it to heart and quickly shrugged it off.

As the two walked back to the office, they spotted a poster for *The King and I* showing at the Uris Theatre. Joey asked Anne if she liked that kind of thing. "Of course!" she quickly responded as he opened one of the big glass doors to let her enter their building. Joey didn't waste any time asking her if he could take her to the play this weekend. She repeated the same line to seal the deal–"Of course!" As the two continued their conversation, they completely forgot about keeping a lid on their encounter. In fact, this time, Joey walked Anne all the way to her desk before getting her phone number and saying good-bye.

She'd have to tell her parents about Joey sometime before he picked her up for the play on Saturday.

15

NOWADAYS Anne was practically cursing the speed of mail travel across the Atlantic. But on Halloween night, Anne's father arrived home a bit later from work and dropped a letter next to her plate as they gathered around the dinner table that evening.

Oh dear, she thought to herself... I'm hungry for dinner but first want to consume the contents of this letter.

On the other hand, she didn't want to appear too eager, as her parents were obviously gauging her reaction at that moment. She thanked her father for the handoff and promptly placed the letter under her plate to read later in her room. She consciously thought of it (and Grant) as "dessert" and immediately found herself blushing uncontrollably at the table.

This time it was her mother who spoke up. "What do you hear from that gentleman in Scotland these days?" The question was so matter-of-fact that Anne wondered if her mother actually thought Grant was simply sending along his daily itinerary or clippings from the Glasgow newspaper.

"Oh, well . . . we are still getting to know more about each other through these letters. He writes in brief, but they are newsy enough."

Nothing more was said, as Anne's father promptly changed the subject to request that Ruth pick up something he needed at the grocery next time she went.

As she finished dinner, Anne offered to help with cleanup, but her mother uncharacteristically released her to read the mail. Anne dashed off to her room down the long hallway that ran through the center of the apartment and once again flopped onto her bed after closing the door.

With greater patience this time, she carefully opened the letter with her index finger and removed the contents—and a small photograph of Grant slipped out the side onto her bed. Her heart soared as she looked at the picture, almost forgetting there was a letter as well. Grabbing the paper, she read:

Sweet Anne,

Your letter arrived at a time when I needed it most. It confirmed in my own heart and mind that you have not forgotten me, despite the great distance. Like you, I have a hard time tearing myself away from the practice of reading your letter over and over again. Somehow it provides me with a sense of connection to you. Besides, I love the smell that still lingers on the paper.

Allow me to address your questions and news in the order they present in your letter to me:

1. Translating for you, I am 6 feet and 2 inches tall and weighing about 200 lbs. I could stand to lift weight for better fitness—perhaps about 100 to 105 lbs. And don't think for a minute that only American men are interested in a woman's measurements.

2. How great that you have found work. I am happy for you. However, I suppose that means you'll be tied to New York for a livelihood, even though you admitted that you don't much like the city. I have never travelled beyond the Isles, and New York City has a romantic attraction to most of us over here.

3. I have been working with my dad for the last three years now. It's something he was hoping I would do at a much earlier age, but that's a long story. Prior to learning this work (mostly on the job, but also from growing up watching him tinker at his workbench at home), I spent several years labouring on a factory line. Without formal education, there's not much available to a wild-eyed young man. Through it all, I've had my music though.

4. Speaking of music, I do plink about on the piano. However, I must go to visit my parents to find one to practise on these days. And from one of my bandmates, I am learning a bit of the fiddle, though I don't own one of those either. I enjoy singing with the group at some of the local establishments around town. I also like to write songs, and you've inspired a few as of late. I've always loved music. My father (George) has a great voice but doesn't use it much anymore, except for singing hymns in church on Sunday. My mom (Mary) tries to get him to sing to her, as he apparently did when they were younger.

5. Sports? I've played some football (we have a few variants on that theme here), shinty, and cricket. But I can bring no shame to my ancestors by staying away from the golf game. I would hardly call myself an athlete since I've not been a serious player of anything but my music. What sport does a 5'2" and 100 lbs. lady play?

I have inserted a photo of myself, though it is about a year old and not much to look at. I only send it along in order to get a photo of you in return. I should treasure it as second best to actually being able to look at you in person. Right now I have to close my eyes to see you standing in front of me.

Now here is my plan to see you again: My parents will soon be writing to your parents to request you visit with us this Christmastime. Of course, you'll be a guest in their home, but I will see you every day there. I realize there is an expense to this, but none for you outside of the round-trip air passage. I am praying that your parents will accede to let you come spend time with us during this wonderful holiday in Scotland. We will take good care of you, and nothing else could I possibly want for Christmas than to see you again. Please come to me.

Affectionately,

Grant

16

ANNE spent an entire mid-November day at work wondering if she should prepare her parents for the letter to come or just wait for them to receive it and gauge their reaction. It was difficult to concentrate at her desk—something Nick couldn't help but notice. He stopped by to ask how she was doing, and that was not his typical routine. She looked up at him and admitted to being distracted today given some news she had received from a friend overseas. He put his hand on her shoulder and gave it a squeeze, offering up a "Well, let me know if I can be of any help, Anne."

Nick was a good boss, but she wasn't sure how he might deal with a request for time off in December, when she would not have been with the company for even ninety days. She had no access to any vacation time, but perhaps he'd let her be gone for a time without pay.

There was no doubt in her mind that she wanted to see Grant—and she reminded herself that she would have made enough money to pay her own way to Scotland by December.

But just as she was contemplating the time and the money, Joey stopped by and rapped on her desk like one would knock on your front door.

"Hey there, what's got you so deep in thought today? I hope it's something we can talk about over lunch," he hinted.

Anne shifted in her chair and said, "Yes, Joey, it is something we should talk about over lunch. I'll meet you out in the lobby at noon."

Joey flashed the thumbs-up sign and dashed off toward the mailroom.

Anne pulled out a pocket calendar she had in her purse to check the dates she might travel. She circled Friday, December 23, as the date she could travel after working that day. Then there was the three-day weekend of Christmas. If she could just get Nick to agree to let her have two more days off work, she figured she could be back at her desk on the twenty-ninth. It was a very short visit, but anything over those four nights in the Donaldson home seemed like a tipping point of overstaying her welcome anyway.

Stuffing the calendar back in her purse, she glanced at her watch, which indicated she had but one hour to get some work done while also figuring out how she was going to tell Joey about her trip.

They'd had a fun time together over dinner and that wonderful Broadway play, after he met her parents when he came to pick her up at the apartment. Not only that, he had tipped his hand about doing something together over the upcoming four-day Thanksgiving holiday. She sensed this might not be easy, but she was also not going to play games with her new friend. She quickly sent up a prayer, trying to turn everything over to the Lord. After all, she'd trusted Him fully to order her steps thus far, and she wasn't about to stop trusting Him now.

As Anne boarded the bus home that evening, she replayed the lunch with Joey over in her mind. The fact that he'd practically given her an ultimatum to choose between him and "this Grant fellow" was a sure sign that he was more serious than she'd realized. On the walk back to the office, she found herself apologizing to Joey about whether he'd gotten the impression that they were in an exclusive relationship. She told him that she appreciated his friendship and hoped they would continue to be friends. However, with a chilly good-bye, Joey took a right at the first hallway once they were inside their office area, leaving Anne to return to her desk alone.

While on the bus ride home, Anne had concluded that she would simply allow the letter to arrive and tell her parents she'd pay her way and accept the invite of the Donaldson family. She knew that if this was something God had intended, nothing would stop her from seeing Grant again. But her heart ached a bit at the realization that the converse was also true. For if He didn't intend for her to see Grant again, something would prevent it from happening.

No sooner had she pushed open the apartment door than Anne heard her mother call her name from the kitchen. For some reason, it always grated on Anne to have someone yell to her like that. It was particularly irritating after a long day at work. Without responding, she proceeded to take off her coat and walk quietly down the hall to the kitchen.

She was a bit surprised to see both of her parents standing in the long and narrow kitchen; a meeting of three now made it feel quite crowded. Her father was holding a letter in his hand, so there was now no doubt in Anne's mind what this conversation would entail. Ken Ledwell had his serious face on and proceeded to ask if she was "involved in this scheme."

She'd long since learned that it didn't work not to come clean with your attorney, so she responded with a point of correction.

"It's not a scheme; it's an invitation—and yes, Grant's last letter did indicate this would be forthcoming."

Her father looked over at her mother as if it was now up to her to dissuade her daughter. Ruth pleaded, "But dear, you don't really know what you're getting into here. And we feel like you've put us on the spot. And besides, what about that young man at work who seems to have taken a liking to you?"

Anne's frustration was reaching a pitch now. "Let me be perfectly clear that I did not instigate this invitation and would never be so forward. Secondarily, you two aren't being asked to deliver your daughter into the hands of strangers. This family has been a member of Pastor McGinty's church for a lifetime. They know their son cannot invite me to his place, so they are opening their home as a neutral location for us to get to know each other better. I have no idea what their letter says, but I'm certain they are simply asking for your blessing upon me to enjoy their hospitality for a few days over the holiday. And as for Joey, we're just friends."

Anne was shocked at what was coming out of her mouth. She searched her mind for the last time she'd made such a cogent argument before her lawyer father. But she was snapped back to reality when her father asked a question so pointed that it almost felt like a knife running through her.

"Are you in love with this man?" he asked. It took her breath away that he would be so bold.

"I don't know the answer to that very big question," Anne responded, "but I know it will go unanswered unless I see him again. And, frankly, I don't want to go through life without getting an answer to that question."

With that she turned and hurried to her bedroom and closed the door. For now her bedroom was a refuge, and it was in that room on that night that Anne realized she had more fight in her for seeing Grant again than she'd ever had for anything in her lifetime. The realization startled her because she knew she'd never felt that strongly about any man before.

The next morning Anne was running late for work, but she downed a bit more coffee before rushing to put on her coat and get out the door to the bus. Her mother was in the kitchen and reminded Anne that last night's conversation wasn't over. Oh dread, Anne thought. It was going to be a long day into night between asking her boss for time off then dealing with her parents over the dinner conversation.

17

ONE of the things Anne was working on for her boss was booking travel for him to Los Angeles for the following month. In that process she'd struck up a good working relationship with Janet, the agent the company used for this purpose. This morning she had to place a call to Janet to get some information on a rental car for Nick, so she decided to call in a favor. (Janet had made an error the week before on a detail that Anne had picked up on, saving Janet many headaches on her end.)

"What can you tell me about airfare to Scotland, Janet?"

Returning to the apartment that evening after work, Anne felt she had her ducks in a row for that discussion with her parents. Hanging her coat on the hall tree, she went directly to the kitchen to offer assistance to her mother on dinner preparations. She was somewhat surprised to find her mom was carrying a brown paper bag to the table. She asked Anne to bring three plates. Turns out, her father was already at the table and ready to pass judgment on the Chinese takeout that mother had brought from a shop a few blocks away. "Well, this is different," Anne stated as cheerfully as she could.

As the three raised their heads from saying grace over the meal, Anne's father was the first to speak.

"I'd like to return to the matter of this letter we've received from the Donaldsons. Your mother and I have decided that if you feel this is something you must do, we can't stop you. We will miss having you here at Christmastime, so the round-trip airfare will have to be our gift to you this year. Of course, all of this is contingent upon your being able to get off work for this trip, and I'd expect you might have some difficulties there. However, that issue may be a factor in keeping the visit short, which I also recommend. After all, what if you don't find this Grant to be the real deal, and you're uncomfortable in their home? You'll need an early out in that event, so keep it short."

Anne couldn't believe what she was hearing! She tried to respond as calmly to her father as he had been in his pronouncement.

"Well, I am very pleasantly surprised at the early Christmas gift. I was prepared to use my own funds for this purpose, so thank you both very much," she said.

"As it turns out, I just happen to work with a travel agent on the job who has given me some details on travel and costs to Scotland. And, though my boss couldn't provide me with any vacation time prior to my having completed six months on the job, he did agree to allow me two days off without pay. If I depart after work on Friday, December 23, I will arrive there on Christmas Eve. And since the day after Christmas is a paid holiday for me, that leaves me my two days off without pay. I can be in Scotland Saturday through Tuesday, travel home on Wednesday, and be back at my desk on the Thursday morning after Christmas."

Winking at her father, she asked, "Is that short enough for you?"

Ken smiled and nodded his approval and then recommended that Anne respond to the Donaldsons directly, since she was the invitee.

Sitting at her desk that night, Anne knew she'd be writing to Grant's parents ... but she also wanted desperately to write to Grant. Should she write him first, or should she respond to them, and he would learn of the trip from them? Oh, how she wished she could confer with Grant directly. Wait—he had given her his phone number on that piece of paper on their one and only date! But she thought better of that due to the expense of such a call and to remembering her upbringing about girls not calling boys on the phone. No, she'd have to make this decision on her own.

Late into the night Anne wrote and rewrote two letters. She had decided to mail them both at the same time. Perhaps both Grant and his parents would simultaneously learn of her plan to return to Scotland and visit their home. She'd leave that to God and the ways of the mail services in both countries.

My Grant,

I am sorry for the delay in writing, but I have great news! After some negotiations with my parents about the invitation to visit you and your family at Christmas, it is now a matter of my booking the flights and counting the days. And I assure you, I will be counting the days to see you again. I have so many questions for you, and I can hardly wait to meet your family.

I have also been able to obtain a few days off of work, but the stay in Glasgow will be short. We must make the best of every hour we have together. I should fly on December 23 from

New York through London to arrive at Edinburgh airport the next afternoon—Christmas Eve. I hope that isn't going to be too disruptive for your family traditions and plans. I will need to depart Scotland on Wednesday the December 28 so that I can return to my job the next day. Those days with you will be precious to me because I will be able to see, hear, and perhaps even get close enough to smell and taste you!

I will send the flight, airline, and arrival time information to you as soon as I have the tickets in hand. Meanwhile, I will also send your parents a letter to confirm this information and thank them for the invitation. Seeing you again will be the perfect Christmas gift!

Soon,

Anne

PS: Thank you for including your photo. I have enclosed mine to you.

Dear Mr. & Mrs. Donaldson,

My parents have shared your invitation letter with me, and they have approved my travel to Glasgow! Thank you for your hospitality, and I am looking forward to getting to know the entire family. Please do not change anything about your usual plans and family traditions on account of me. I will try to be a low-maintenance houseguest.

I have written to Grant as well to let him know that I will purchase air passage to depart after my workday on December 23. That will put me in Edinburgh airport on the afternoon of Christmas Eve. I will need to return to that airport for my departure flight on Wednesday, as I am required back at my job the morning of December 29. It is a short visit, but I am already looking forward to every minute.

I will submit the flight arrival time and other particulars to Grant once I've secured my tickets. I am assuming he will meet me at the airport to take me to your home, but if I need to make other arrangements, I ask that you instruct me on that.

Thank you again for the invitation. I am counting the days!

Warm regards,

Anne Ledwell

18

KEN LEDWELL often conceded to his beloved wife when it came to cooking versus eating out. Thanksgiving would apparently be no different. Anne was really hoping for a home-cooked meal, and even offered to attempt to make the feast on her own, but her mother promptly injected, "Better to make reservations than turkey dinner!"

It was a chilly but lovely evening on the town, with dinner at a swanky new restaurant on East 49th in Manhattan. Since Anne's father had given up on owning a car in the city just months after moving there from Jersey, he shelled out the money for a cab each way tonight. The ladies got dressed up, and everyone felt like a stuffed turkey after eating so much food.

As the cab made its way back to their apartment, Anne was staring out the backseat window at the lights, the skyscrapers, and the people on the streets. She was grateful that this difficult town had gotten through the humid summer of a blackout, infamous crime, a police corruption scandal, and a contentious mayoral election. And though she was a Dodgers fan, she had to admit that it had been fun watching the New York boys of summer take the pennant this year. In the end, she was starting to understand why her father called the city "an exciting crummy place."

New York really was alive and kicking, despite the mass exodus of residents in the last decade or so. She could relate to that exodus, because this wasn't something she would ever have chosen for herself, yet here she was, living and working in the city that never sleeps.

Soon her thoughts turned to wondering what it was like for Grant to live in his big city of Glasgow. It's all relative, she thought to herself, but she couldn't help but wonder if he really liked it there. Well, soon she would have an answer to that question too. Just thirty days from now she'd be seeing that muscular city through his eyes.

Thousands of miles away, there was no Thanksgiving holiday, so Grant received regular mail delivery—and it was exactly what he was hoping for. "She's comin' ... she's really comin' back!" he shouted at Mrs. McBride from across the kitchen that night. "An look here, Mrs. M ... this is what she looks like." He showed off the small photograph that had slipped out of the envelope and onto the kitchen counter.

"She's a beauty to be sure, Grant—and a wee thing," said Mrs. McBride after plucking the photo out of his fingers to get a closer look. He had an urge to grab it right back from her but waited patiently for her to hand it over. He sat down to stare at the photo and reread the brief letter several times. His mind was racing. It wouldn't be long now ... a month, and he'd be able to hold her in his arms again.

19

ANNE was trying hard to stay focused at the workplace, and she wondered if Grant was trying to do the same. It was now mid-December, and she hadn't heard anything in response to her two letters mailed on the same day. What if they didn't arrive? What if they'd changed their minds? Oh, her inner voice was working overtime today.

She took a deep breath and started reading the financial prospectus in her hand that she just couldn't seem to concentrate on. How was she ever going to learn this business if she couldn't stay focused long enough to get through this dreadfully boring document? Maybe she should just go to the lunchroom and eat. Yes, it was noon—and she'd take the material with her to read while she ate her lunch.

Grant was exiting the back of the repair shop late this evening, taking care to make sure everything was locked and secured for the night. His father had departed hours ago, but at least he'd remembered to bring the letter that Anne had sent. Grant had asked several times to see it because his father had not been forthcoming with the contents, other than to tell Grant that he should write to her to confirm he'd be picking her up at the airport on Christmas Eve. As if he needed prompting to write to Anne. Why, he had already mailed that letter days ago.

Dear Anne,

That was a short letter you sent, but it contained the very words I wanted to read—that you are going to come to me! My heart soared to see those words then flew even higher to see your photograph. I am captive to your beauty. That's what my landlady said about you when I showed her your picture—you're a beauty.

By the time you receive this letter, it may be only a week before we are together again. I will call ahead to the airport to confirm the flight from London into Edinburgh, and I promise to be at the gate to pick you up on the afternoon of Christmas Eve. My parents are looking forward to having you in their home, and you will be well cared for. And, of course, I will look after you every moment we are together. Please assure your parents of this.

There will be no shortage of things to do and see during this too-short visit. Anne, I can't even begin to tell you how happy (and excited) I am that my plan has come together so that we can come together.

Godspeed you to me,

Grant

The next morning when Grant returned to open the shop, his eyes passed over the calendar in the office. This had become a daily ritual to him as he counted the days for Anne to arrive. It was now December 16, and she would be boarding a plane in just one week. As he stared at the calendar in the office, he didn't even realize that his father had walked in until he barked, "Get past your daydreamin', man—it's time ta get ta work on those clocks Damian brought in yesterday."

Grant was a bit startled but definitely used to his father giving him a hard time. It seemed to be the way the old man expressed his love for his son. In days gone by, when he was a teen, Grant had found it discouraging and disheartening—enough to keep them apart for many years. But things were different now because Grant had learned to forgive ... and so had his father. So, the chiding turned from being a hindrance in their relationship to an odd sort of "love language" they had with each other.

George Donaldson switched on the overhead light in the office and then tossed an envelope onto the desk where Grant had momentarily settled. It was a telegram—obvious from its markings. "Well, it may be addressed ta me, but I thought you should see it," his father stated very matter-of-factly.

Grant slipped the notice out of the envelope to read: Anne arriving at Edinburgh 14:20 on Dec. 24th Flight 26 from London. From: Kenneth Ledwell.

20

ANNE had worked hard all day finishing up several tasks for Nick, who would be on vacation for two weeks starting tomorrow. Of course she also had numerous items she needed to bring to a close involving her own work before she would board her flight tonight to Scotland. It felt surreal to think that she'd be seeing Grant tomorrow!

A few of her single female co-workers knew what she was up to and kept stopping by her desk. Seems they wanted to know more about how she met this guy, and if he had a single brother. However, Nick's executive assistant, Julia, was quite suspicious of this trip. She was an older divorcée who seemed to have a bit of a chip on her shoulder. Julia thought perhaps Anne was being naïve about this whole thing and would likely get her heart broken. Just to bring that thought home, she leaned over Anne's desk and whispered, "Kinda like Joey, who's now reduced to going out with Missy in Accounting. You know you broke his heart, don't you?"

Anne had considered the possibility of disappointment the first time Julia spoke to her like that about men, but neither cynicism nor the potential for heartbreak would keep her from getting one more opportunity to be with and know Grant. She reminded herself once again today that if God wanted this to happen, nothing would stop it from happening. So far, nothing was stopping her.

Practically bounding into the apartment after work that dark winter evening, Anne heard her mother's query from the bedroom: "Do you need any help with last-minute packing? The cab will be here at 6:00 p.m. sharp for you!"

Anne looked down at her watch only to realize she had just twenty minutes to change clothes, brush her teeth, and sit on the lid of her suitcase to snap it shut.

"I'll be ready!" she hollered back.

Scurrying around from the bathroom to her bedroom to the kitchen, she was finally ready at 5:55 p.m. Her parents were starting to hover over her, asking the usual questions: Had she remembered to take the converter? Did she have her round-trip tickets? What about her passport?–and a million other things.

Stuffing an apple into her purse, Anne announced from the kitchen that she was heading out the door—only to find her parents were already at the door. Anne hugged her mother, whose only commentary was that she thank her hosts, and be careful.

"Have a great Christmas, Mom. I'll tell you all about mine when I return!" exclaimed Anne.

Her father insisted on riding the elevator down and seeing that she got safely into the cab. On the way down, he told her that he'd sent a telegram to the Donaldson home with her flight information. What a caring thing for him to do, Anne thought. She proceeded to give him a big hug just as the doors opened at the ground floor.

Ben left early this evening to start his holiday vacation, so Ken Ledwell opened all doors and helped Anne with her suitcase. Getting her situated in the cab, he confirmed her destination with the cabbie, who nodded and answered, "Yes, sir." Anne waved at her dad as the car pulled away from the curb and drove off into the cold night.

21

THE flight to London seemed smooth so far, outside of a baby crying off and on at the rear of the plane during the night. It had been very difficult for Anne to sleep during the transatlantic portion of the flight. The seat was uncomfortable, and she just couldn't seem to shut down her brain. Being this excited meant sleep intervals that probably lasted only one to two hours at a time and became even shorter as she noticed the first light of the next day filtering through the closed windows of the plane. It wouldn't be long now, she thought. But the drone of the engines faded away one more time as she caught her last hours of sleep before a flight attendant brought around coffee, tea, and breakfast.

The heavyset man in the seat next to her had nudged her to see if she wanted anything, and she was glad he had. She was both hungry and thirsty. She had earlier noticed that her seatmate was an older gentleman with a large metal crucifix hanging from his neck inside of his jacket. Perhaps he was making some kind of pilgrimage, she thought, because the large jewelry was not the kind of thing most men would be comfortable wearing. While they ate breakfast the man told her about his intended visit to a shrine in Ireland—something he'd done once before. But it was not just his Catholic faith that drew him there for he also had family in Derry. He then asked Anne what her business was in Edinburgh which she had already indicated was her final destination. She hesitated a bit for lack of a good way to describe her visit but eventually characterized it as spending the holidays with friends. That seemed to satisfy her seatmate, who didn't ask any more probing questions.

Having easily made her connecting flight to Edinburgh after a short layover at London's Heathrow airport, this leg of the trip seemed to go so quickly that there was no time for additional sleep. As the pilot issued final approach instructions to passengers and crew, Anne's heart was racing. She had reached down under the seat in front of her to grab her handbag and touch up her sleepy hair and makeup in the small mirror she kept there. Before stowing it away, she pulled out her small photo of Grant one more time. Just think, within minutes she'd see him in the flesh! Anne sent up a final prayer, asking the Lord to help her to be a gracious guest—and thanking Him for bringing her thus far. She almost pinched herself to see if it was real but instead pinched her cheeks to bring on the color.

The cold air cut through Anne as she exited the plane to walk down the stairs. Her eyes darted back and forth from the steps in front of her to the glass windows of the airport, in hopes of catching a glimpse of the man. She wondered if he had spotted her. She walked single file through the door with the other passengers and could hear their chatter as they were directed to a passport control and customs holding area.

How unromantic, she thought, that there's no way to meet family and friends when you arrive. The process was one she was used to from all her travels, so it had never bothered her before. Now it was a complete irritant, but she tried not to let it show to the officers simply doing their jobs. One of them even winked at her as he returned her stamped passport to her.

Finally free to walk through the door marked EXIT TO CLAIM BAGGAGE, she felt herself speeding up, as if to escape. She couldn't be sure, but as she crossed the door threshold, she thought she saw Grant standing tall in the distance with his arms folded across his big chest. Moving even faster, her mind confirmed what she was seeing with her eyes at the very moment he opened those strong arms wide to scoop her up and turn the two of them away from the crowd.

"Thank God you're here with me naw," Grant whispered in her ear as he gently placed her feet on the ground again. In that moment she felt so secure and warm that she didn't ever want to release him. And, as it turns out, he didn't seem to want to release her either—except to cup both of his hands around her face to tilt it toward his. He proceeded to kiss her softly on the lips, and then the cheek, and finally the top of her head. As he drew her close again, she was finally able to speak without risking tears.

"I've missed you, Grant."

He grabbed her hand and pointed to the baggage area, as if to say, let's get out of here.

Grant's stride placed him at the trunk of his car to put her suitcase there, while Anne was just catching up to him. He opened her car door while asking her about the flight. She claimed it was fine and that she was glad that part of the trip was behind her. As he bounded into the driver's seat on the right-hand side of the car, he placed the key in the ignition and then shifted his entire body toward her.

Placing his left arm over the back of her seat, he reached his right hand around the back of her neck to draw her to his lips again. This was to be no gentle kiss, but rather a long and involved one. Anne felt herself melting away. As their bliss ended, Grant drew in a deep breath and began to speak very intentionally, almost as though he'd rehearsed.

"Anne, I need ta tell you right naw that I'm in love with you. By that, I don't mean ta rush things, I jes want you ta know that it's all become pearfectly clear ta me durin' this time we've been apart. I know I can't expect you ta feel the same way for me, but I needed ta lay it out in this moment."

A peace came over Anne as she realized that "this moment" was the answer to the question she had brought with her over these thousands of miles. In a measured voice, while trying desperately to maintain self-control, she responded, "You are the answer to my question, Grant. I know now that I do love you. In fact, no matter what's to become of us, I suspect I will go to my grave in love with you. Should we never be together, I pity the man who would have to settle for a shadow of what I feel for you."

As she finished her sentence, she noticed the catch in her voice. He noticed it too and put both arms around her to hold her tightly. They lingered in this quiet embrace for a long time before Grant released her and turned to start the car.

All the way from the airport to his family home in Glasgow, Grant explained how they would spend their days together, starting with Christmas Eve supper this evening. His eyes danced as he described his mother's great cooking. He stopped his train of thought to point out sights along the way, while Anne studied his profile as he spoke, noting dimples when he smiled broadly.

As they approached Glasgow, Anne took her eyes off Grant long enough to notice several large skyscrapers huddled together in the distance. The outcropping of such tall buildings in the middle of what seemed like nowhere was odd enough that she inquired about them. Grant explained that they were called the Red Road Flats, and his oldest sister and her young family lived there. He went on to tell Anne that there had been a fire in one of the towers just a few months earlier, in which a little boy had perished. "I hope Gwen can move from there someday. I jes don't feel it's a safe place."

As the afternoon sun poured through the car windows, Anne also noticed Grant's five o'clock shadow, which revealed even more reddish hair coloring than she saw in his eyebrows. She was hanging on his every word, but her eyes were working overtime to take him in. To her, he was the most handsome man she'd ever seen. Lost in that thought, those very words fell out of her mouth before she realized what she was saying. Grant laughed as he attempted to continue his litany of the days to come, brushing off the compliment with, "Aw there, lass, pearhaps it's true that love is blind!"

22

ANNE wasn't sure what to expect as Grant drove through the typical urban social housing one would see in European cities. She didn't know if she should be looking for a tenement or row home, but eventually Grant pulled up to a small single-family home just outside of the city proper. The driveway consisted of two concrete runners with grass growing in between them, and Grant continued on that path to the back of the property, where he parked near what looked like a combination of garage and barn structure. "Well, welcome ta our humble home, Anne. I'll get your bag."

As she got out of the car, Anne saw a stocky older woman wearing an apron over her plain dress opening the back door and waving at them. "That's ma mam," Grant nodded to Anne. "Let me introduce you."

As they approached his mother, Anne was struck by how much she reminded her of her own maternal grandmother, who had passed away just a few years earlier. She wondered how much older Grant's mother was than her own mother, for she appeared to be at least a decade older. Thin and graying hair outlined her smiling face.

Before Grant got a word of introduction out, Mary Donaldson reached out her hand to Anne. In taking Anne's hand, Mary proceeded to pull Anne toward her to hug her instead. Anne felt so welcome just standing on the small slab porch.

"Come in, dearie, it's guid ta meet you. I want you ta meet Grant's faither an sister."

Once inside the warm, cozy home, Anne was standing squarely in front of George Donaldson and knew immediately from whence Grant's size and stature came. George was apparently not the hugging type, but he did hold out his big hand to greet her warmly. As he did, he turned her over to Gena Donaldson, Grant's younger sister, who was just coming out of the small kitchen.

Gena shook Anne's hand in a fairly businesslike manner and greeted her in what sounded to Anne like a much shallower Scottish accent than the rest of the family.

With introductions made, Mary informed Anne that she'd be staying in Grant's boyhood room and instructed Grant to put Anne's suitcase there. Grant led the way down the narrow hallway just off the main living area. Following right behind was a curious Gena, who was Anne's age. (Given that Grant was the middle child and twenty-eight years old, Anne speculated that Gena might have been a surprise baby who came along when the older Donaldson couple were least expecting it!)

The close quarters in the small room was something noticeable to Anne, though not so much to these siblings who had grown up with little space and few belongings. The room had all the appearance of long-since being stripped of boyish items or toys. Clearly Mrs. Donaldson had repurposed the small room for a single guest, due to the one twin bed that ran nearly the length of the small room.

Grant seemed annoyed that his little sister was present and appeared to be putting off something he wanted to say to Anne. Gena filled the silence by ordering him out of the room to help their mother by replenishing the wood supply for the fireplace. Grant returned the order by demanding that Gena show Anne the rest of the home and where the one household bathroom was located.

With that, Gena did as she was instructed, showing Anne a glimpse of the room where she was sleeping over the holiday. That room was still quite girly, and Gena explained that growing up, she and her older sister had shared the room until Gwen got married and moved away. The bathroom was right across the small dark hall from Anne's room, so she took this opportunity to freshen up and agreed to rejoin Gena in the living area.

Within minutes of emerging from the darker part of the small home, Anne entered the light-filled living room where Grant was working the fireplace into higher flames. Mr. Donaldson claimed to be "supervising" Grant's work from his easy chair, which was next to the small Christmas tree in the corner.

Aside from two candles in the large front window of the home, Anne didn't see much evidence of Christmas decoration about the house. To the right of the front door (which was easy enough to see from the back door due to the smallness of the home) was a corner with a long table and bench seats on each side, with two chairs at either end. To the right of that space was apparently the kitchen, as Mrs. Donaldson was coming out of the doorless entry bringing several mugs ringed around her fingers.

She beckoned Anne and Grant to join her at the table for tea. She made one more trip into the kitchen, emerging with a pot of hot tea. "Do you take anything in your tea, Anne?" she queried.

"Yes, ma'am, if you have milk or cream on hand," Anne responded. This time it was Gena who spoke out from the kitchen, indicating she'd bring it with her.

As all the ladies were seated at the table, Grant joined in by straddling the bench so he could face Anne as she sat properly on the bench. With his fist propping up his chin, he stared at her. Without taking his eyes off her, he said, "Naw you see with your own eyes what I've been sayin' all along, Mam. She's a beauty."

Mary Donaldson agreed but chided him for "embarrassin' the lass."

Gena chimed in with the first questions for Anne: What was New York City like? Did she like living there? How did she afford it there? What was it like to shop there?

Clearly, thought Anne, that was the fascination for Gena—her American ways. That was probably also why Gena had toned down her accent to sound less Scottish! How Anne wished to influence her new acquaintance to appreciate what she had and her own uniqueness.

After about an hour of chatting and nothing but cold tea in the pot, Mrs. Donaldson declared her need to finish up in the kitchen. Anne offered to help, but Mary showed her the kitchen and declared there was only room enough for one cook in the small area. She took Anne's hand and thanked her for coming to spend Christmas with them. She then placed Anne's hand into Grant's as he stood there taking up the entire doorway.

Anne took notice that Mr. Donaldson had vacated his chair, and Grant offered that his father had gone to his workshop in that separate building she'd seen out in the back of the property. That gave him an excuse to take her outside to show her around.

They exited out the back door into the cold and darkening evening. As they approached a muddy spot, Grant took the opportunity to sweep her up in his arms to carry her. Though she protested a bit, she thrilled at his attention—and at getting another kiss as he carried her all the way into the building.

It was part garage (where the Donaldson car was parked) and part storage, but off to one side she could see light spilling out from the large gap under a door. Grant opened the door, and there was the "old man" standing over a high workbench filled with tools of his trade, as well as clock parts and pieces. Pulling up a high stool, Grant lifted Anne by her tiny waist to perch her there.

The two men talked a bit about business and customers as though she wasn't there. It didn't take long to observe their bantering, which had a certain edge to it. This wasn't how Anne's father spoke to her, but she chalked it up to communications being different between father and son. She, after all, had no brothers and nothing to which she could compare. But soon their conversation came to a close, and Grant lifted her off the chair to the floor.

The couple said their good-byes and walked down the driveway to the front of the property, where Anne could see more of the house and the neighborhood. As Grant was pointing things out, a car turned into the driveway. It was his sister, Gwen, and her family, who were there for Christmas Eve dinner. Grant reminded Anne that they lived on the other side of

Glasgow town, in the tower flats she had noticed during their drive from the airport.

Anne was introduced to Gwen and her husband, Keith, and their active twin five-year-old sons—Jon and Ennis. As they all went back into the house via the front door, the boys squeezed in between the adults to enter first. They were pretty excited to see their grandparents, uncle, and auntie—and the Christmas tree—and Jon took the time to tug on Grant's sleeve to ask if he had brought his guitar with him. Disappointed with the negative response, Jon took off out the back door after his brother, who had already been told to retrieve their grandfather from the workshop.

Anne saw that the table was dressed, and the feast was taking shape. After lots of catching-up talk, everyone gravitated to the fireplace that warmed the main portion of the house. Anne took this opportunity to slip back to her much colder guest room to retrieve some gifts she had brought for the family.

It was Grant who noticed her absence and went looking for her. His tall frame stood in the doorway to his old bedroom as he asked if he could enter.

"Of course—it's your room, after all!"

Grant came into the small space and admitted that he just wanted to be alone with her. She smiled and put her arms around his neck as they talked about their newly proclaimed love—reveling in it together. Within minutes they heard the dinner call from his father's deep and gruff voice, and Anne gathered up the gifts. She placed them on the bench seat of the console piano in the living room and joined hands with Grant to sit down together at the dinner table.

With his mother and father at either end of the table, the rest of the family was packed tightly on the benches. As the boys were being shushed by their father, Mr. Donaldson asked Grant to say grace on this Christmas Eve. Anne was looking forward to the prayer, and just listening to Grant's beautiful brogue.

"Our Lord and our God, we gather together tanight ta celebrate the proclaimin' of the bairn Christ. May He be reborn in our hearts this night, and may we ever be grateful for the precious gift first given for us. Bless this food ta us for strenth, and bless the family—those near an far. This year we thank you for bringin' Anne safely ta us. I thank you for her. And for all your great gifts ta us, we humbly thank you. Amen."

The meal on the table was simple but plentiful, and Anne was definitely hungry! While the adults were passing food and eating, the twins were already voicing their excitement about Christmas. They sheepishly asked their grandfather if they might open their gifts tonight. The old man sternly reminded them that the family tradition was that gift-giving took place only on Christmas morning. The boys sighed and then whined.

Besides, their grandfather inquired, what made them so certain there would be gifts for them? That question caused the two to pipe down, if only to contemplate the horrible possibility of no gifts for them.

Anne learned that the Byrnes would be leaving after dinner for Gwen's in-laws' home in the upland. Once dinner was over and they had departed, the rest of the family would pile in the car to drive to church for the Christmas Eve candlelight service. Anne was looking forward to returning to that little church where she had first laid eyes on the handsome singer who now sat so close to her, she could feel his warmth.

Anne felt like she was rising above the table and listening in to this conversation as a spectator. The family's ease with each other, and their love for one another, was evident. She was jerked back to reality when she heard Grant say that he wanted to walk her home after church so he could show her where he lived.

Mrs. Donaldson shot a disapproving glance his way, saying, "You have her reputation ta consider, Grant. A man aught not take a lady ta his apartment at night alone, lest people talk."

Grant started to protest, but his father cut him off with a curt, "She's jes after tellin' you."

Anne wasn't sure what that phrase meant, but she could tell it was Mr. Donaldson's final thought on the matter.

Grant relented, especially since Gena reminded him that he could take Anne to see his place when he drove Gena back to school the next day. Gena winked at her brother and said, "That way you'll be seen walkin' into your apartment with two women—in the light of day, no less!"

Anne could tell by the expression on Mary Donaldson's face that she didn't approve of Gena's sarcasm.

As dinner came to a close, Anne realized she was about to violate Mr. Donaldson's edict of no gifts on Christmas Eve. She had something for the Byrnes . . . and for the boys to take with them tonight, since she might not see them again during her short visit. In a soft voice she asked if he might make an exception this one time. The boys squealed, "Yes, please, grandfaither!"

"I suppose this one time," George stated dryly.

Anne left the table to retrieve the gifts she had brought. There were two red-wrapped rectangular boxes—one she handed to Gwen, and the second she placed in front of Mrs. Donaldson. She explained that she'd brought her favorite chocolates made on the west coast of the United States. She'd had to send away for the candy and then brought it with her to Scotland. The ladies thanked her profusely, but the boys seemed a bit disappointed. That was, until Anne brought forth two cellophane-wrapped chocolate-covered marshmallow Christmas trees—the size of their little boy hands. Having now jumped off the bench seat, they went over to hug her and gleefully grab the chocolates.

Mary Donaldson asked them if they were going to want her bread pudding for dessert, or were they going to eat chocolates instead. In unison they yelled, "Both!" Gwen frowned at them and gathered up the marshmallow trees from them for another time. "Aw," they whined—at least until they saw the bread pudding with sauce arriving at the table. Everyone raved over the bread pudding, and Anne couldn't help but notice there was a bit of a kick to the sauce. Now that was different—something her Baptist mother would never do!

As the conversation was winding down and Mary reached out to pick up the plates, Grant stayed her hand and turned to his father saying, "As it is the family tradition not ta open gifts on Christmas Eve, I'll instead do the openin' of a gift I have for Anne." Concerned that Grant was defying his father, Anne started to protest, but Grant raised his index finger to her mouth and then kissed her. Jon and Ennis started saying "ew" right away at the sight of their uncle kissing a girl. Then Grant reached into his shirt pocket, pulled out a black velvet box, and opened it to reveal a beautiful but simple ring with a small diamond solitaire.

Anne took in a deep breath. "Oh, my goodness," she said.

Grant proceeded: "Before God an ma family, I profess ma forever love for you an ask that you marry me, Anne."

Overwhelmed with joy and without hesitation, she responded with, "Of course I will marry you, Grant. Yes—absolutely, yes!"

Now the boys were again off the bench squealing and jumping up and down around the couple. Mrs. Donaldson was smiling through her tears, while Gwen's husband was already reaching over the table to shake Grant's hand. Finally, the patriarch spoke up, and everyone listened.

"The openin' of this gift is the openin' of our family's heart ta you, Anne. Congratulations, Grant, you've chosen well." With that, George Donaldson stretched out his hand to his son.

The household was all abuzz now with talk about this surprise. George Donaldson now knew why Grant had been working late so many evenings. It had to be his labor in trade for the ring, for he knew that Grant could not otherwise have afforded the purchase.

Grant reached for Anne's hand and walked her over to the couch. Sitting down, he patted the empty space next to him to beckon her to sit by his side. She first insisted that she should be helping with the dinner dishes, but his beautiful hazel eyes were more insistent.

As she sat down next to Grant, he put his arm around her and whispered in her ear, "With your yes, you've made me the happiest man in the world tanight."

She turned to him, saying, "And I am happy, Grant—though this comes as a complete surprise. How ever will I tell my parents that within hours of arriving in Scotland, I became engaged to be married?"

Grant laughed and then looked into her big blue eyes and said, "We'll find a way, darlin', we'll find a way."

23

WITH the kids and gifts packed up, the Byrnes drove off into the cold and foggy Christmas Eve, but not before Gwen had given Anne a sisterly embrace and a wish for happiness with her brother. Anne wasn't exactly sure when she'd see Gwen again, but she had a sense that they would become strong supporters of one another going forward.

Soon after their departure, the rest of the family was squeezing into Mr. Donaldson's car to drive to Pastor McGinty's church about a mile away toward town. Anne rather enjoyed being stuffed into the small backseat with Grant—and Gena, of course!

As the church came into view, it looked different to her due to the fog shroud and the dark night. However, it didn't take long for it to feel familiar again when she entered with the family and saw Pastor McGinty mingling with the faithful in the narthex. He saw Anne and pulled her aside to give her a hug and to tell her how he'd heard she was making this return trip. She told him how thrilled she was to be back in his church, but the good parson corrected her with, "Ah, lass, she's God's church. I am jes her tender."

No sooner had the family moved into "their pew" on the right center side of the dividing aisle than the organist started with a prelude in the candlelit sanctuary. Anne noticed that Mr. Donaldson was saving a seat for his wife, who seemed to have disappeared momentarily, but soon she rejoined the family, as the music was coming to a close. Pastor McGinty seemed a bit rushed as he hurried to his seat in the front.

The whole scene seemed unreal to Anne, like a storybook church in a storybook place on this storybook night of Christmas Eve. But the dominant story this night was that of the coming of the Christ-child as read by the pastor from the book of Luke, chapter 2.

It happened that a decree went out at this time from the emperor Augustus, enjoining that the whole world should be registered; this register was the first one made during the time when Cyrinus was governor of Syria. All must go and give in their names, each in his own city; and Joseph, being of David's clan and family, came up from the town of Nazareth, in Galilee, to David's city in Judaea, the city called Bethlehem, to give in his name there. With him was his espoused wife Mary, who was then in her pregnancy; and it was while they were still there that the time came for her delivery. She brought forth a son, her first-born, whom she wrapped in his swaddling-clothes, and laid in a manger, because there was no room for them in the inn.

As Pastor McGinty read on, Anne leaned over to ask Grant what version of scripture the pastor was reading from. Grant whispered back to her, "McGinty loves the Knox Bible for such occasions," to which he added a wink.

The service included a brief exposition of the scripture passage, prayers, and traditional Christmas carols. Anne knew the history of Christmas Day in Scotland and still couldn't bring herself to imagine treating it like any other day by going to work. It made her heart glad to see these Scots celebrating with such fervor on the eve of the Savior's birth.

As the service appeared to be coming to a close, Pastor McGinty moved from his pulpit to be front and center in the sanctuary. He drew something out of his pocket that looked like a braided cord. He proceeded to tell the congregation that he was about to do something he would normally never combine with a Christmas Eve service. However, he went on to tell them that the simple request actually made perfect sense at this time.

He began to remind his audience of an old Scottish tradition that he saw as a picture of Christ's purpose for coming to earth the first time, and that was to give Himself to His bride, the church. The pastor went on to say that a tradition arose in old Scotland owing to the more practical fact that while the English had a parson in almost every town, the Scots didn't. So in those days, it was accepted that a man and woman could announce their intention to marry within a year and a day from a hand-fasting ceremony. Without a parson around, it might be months before the couple could formally wed, so the hand-fasting was a future promise to marry when the next cleric came through the village.

Pastor McGinty was taking great care to explain that this was not intended to be a "trial marriage" for the couple, as they were not to come together until they were officially wed. However, it did signal the betrothal or engagement, with intent to be married. So it is, he explained, with the bride of Christ which is betrothed to Him who will one day take us to the Marriage Feast to be with Him forever. It was a beautiful picture of the spiritual transaction of marriage, and therefore, how important marriage is to God.

With that, Pastor McGinty asked Grant to come to the front and bring Anne with him. Anne felt as though she were frozen in place. Was this really happening? Grant hadn't told her about this. As he stood up and held out his hand to her, and in the space of a second in time, she asked herself if she could trust him. The answer came as she felt herself rise to take his hand and follow his lead to stand by the pastor. While her mind was racing, she barely heard the happy chatter that was coming from the congregation.

Pastor McGinty spoke to the people first, relating the story of how Anne had first seen Grant here in the church when she was visiting with her parents in September. He told the crowd that he had just learned of Grant's proposal of marriage to Anne this evening at the family home and that Anne had accepted and now wore an engagement ring that symbolized her intent to marry Grant at a future time to be determined. Pastor McGinty looked at Anne and asked her if this was true. Anne responded with a quiet "Yes."

The pastor then told the congregation that Grant's mother had offered up a braided cord made of Clan Donaldson tartan for use tonight. That was what he had pulled from his pocket earlier and now held in his hand. Pastor McGinty drew the right hands of the two before him together, Grant clasped Anne's hand in his, and the pastor tied their hands together with the cord.

He turned to Grant and asked, "Do you, Grant Caelen Donaldson, naw publicly announce your intent ta marry Anne Elizabeth Ledwell within a year an a day?"

Grant answered with a strong and sturdy "Aye."

With that, the pastor untied the cord and handed it to Anne, confirming it was a gift from Mr. and Mrs. Donaldson as a sign of her future addition to the family and clan. Putting his hand on the shoulders of Anne and Grant, Pastor McGinty asked the congregation to join him in a prayer of blessing for the couple.

"Faither God, I present Grant an Anne ta you as betrothed ta one another with intent ta wed in the bonds of holy matrimony. May they learn of an care for one another more deeply each day as they approach the blessed day of their wedding. I ask that you keep them in obedience ta you an far from the wiles of the evil one. May they bring honor ta each other, their families, an ta you, naw an forever. Amen."

There was a yip from someone in the crowd, and everyone began clapping as the couple returned to the family pew. With the raising of his hand, the pastor then quieted the audience and proceeded to give the benediction. Then, wishing everyone a merry Christmas, he dismissed his flock into the night.

Just as Anne was about to say something to Grant, she heard the beautiful strains of bagpipes from outside the church. Grant leaned over Anne to give his mom a peck on the cheek and to remind his parents that he would walk Anne straight home.

As they all stood up to put on their coats, hats, and gloves to enter the frigid outdoors, George Donaldson placed his jacket over Anne's shoulders. Patting her head, he said, "Walkin' home, you'll need this more than me, lass!" For a moment, Anne's concerns about what had just happened evaporated, lost in the warmth of her welcoming new family and the extended church family.

Outside and alone at last, Grant and Anne began walking home while listening to the pipes playing outside the church doors. The frozen earth crunched under their feet, but the inner warmth that Anne felt had overtaken her, and tears came to her eyes. With the steady music fading away in the distance, Grant took her small hand in his hand. He was looking ahead and didn't notice the tears until he heard Anne's muffled sniffles.

"There, lassie, are those sad tears or happy tears?" he asked.

Attempting to collect herself, she asked Grant what he knew about the hand-fasting.

"I had no idea that was comin'–I think ma mam was the instigator. I gave ma family a surprise by proposin' ta you tonight at supper, an I suppose she returned the surprise on me!"

No response came from Anne. She was processing all of this in her mind.

"Are you upset with me, Anne?" he asked.

"No, Grant," she answered. "I love you and am very happy. It's just all such a whirlwind for me—everything has happened so fast. I guess I just need some time to adjust to what I never would have seen coming when I boarded a plane in the States not that long ago."

Grant put his arm around her and pulled her close, saying, "More than anythin', I think you need some sleep, lass. I'll get you home, where you'll sleep in ma old bed in ma old room. But you'll not be rid of me for long, because I will return in the mornin' for Christmas breakfast."

They walked on quietly but soon passed a small, run-down cottage with a large tree in the front yard. Grant pointed to the place, which was dark with the exception of a lit candle in the front window. "That's ma place, Anne. Actually, it's Mrs. McBride's place, where I jes rent a room upstairs of the kitchen." Anne just nodded.

Though Anne was so at ease underneath Grant's arm, she was also fatigued. Perhaps it was jet lag, but more likely she'd been operating on very few hours of sleep and was still trying to comprehend how much her life had changed in just this one day.

As they finally approached the front door of the Donaldson home, it was clear everyone else had already bedded down for the night, and the fireplace was but embers now. Inside the dimly lit living room, Grant took his father's overcoat from Anne's shoulders—then he also helped her remove her own coat under that. Placing both coats over the back of the couch, he turned back to Anne to say good night. He embraced her first then took her by the chin and kissed her tenderly.

"We have much ta discuss tomorrow, so you must sleep well. I love you—an can hardly wait ta make you ma guidwife."

With that, he turned her toward the bedroom and quietly let himself out the front door.

Anne fell into bed after putting on her pajamas, and despite her mind racing, she was asleep within minutes.

24

As the first light of day came through the curtain of the small window of her bedroom, Anne began to stretch. Suddenly, she was aware of the ring on her finger, as she wasn't one who wore much jewelry. Holding up her left hand to stare at the beautiful ring through sleepy eyes, she was in awe. How pretty the diamond was, and it was set in what looked like silver or white gold. She was no expert on such things, but it didn't matter the quality or value, she loved its simplicity—and the man who gave it to her. The ring fit perfectly. How did Grant know what size ring she wore?

Anne could hear the floor creaking outside her room, so she knew the family was stirring. Oh yes—it was Christmas morning!

After taking far too long in the bathroom, Anne emerged having washed up. She had even swept her long hair upon her head with some large pins and had put on her favorite pants (a pair her father had always frowned upon: she looked "poured into" them, he said), and an unconstructed white peasant-style blouse with a keyhole tie in the front. She liked the colorful embroidered flowers across the gathered neckline. But since it was a bit sheer (which she thought Grant might like), she wore a pretty cabled cardigan sweater unbuttoned over it.

As she entered the family living room, she was surprised to see Grant was already sitting at the long dining table having tea with his mother. Grant was beaming, and he stood as she approached, and that for the purpose of giving her a great big hug and kiss.

"Guid Christmas mornin'!" Grant pronounced.

"Right back at ya!" she replied. The American lingo seemed to tickle mother and son.

Mary Donaldson was already pouring tea for Anne and telling her that as soon as Gena was awake, they'd be having breakfast. She also announced that later on they could watch the Queen's speech on television. Grant chuckled over that and informed Anne that the ladies of the household seemed to like that tradition, but she could be assured his father would have nothing to do with it. Anne didn't inquire as to why that might be but decided to ask that question of Grant when they were alone.

With a good night's sleep, Anne was back to her self-confident ways. She was looking forward to this day and settled right into the three-way conversation. This was such a special and sweet time with Grant's mother, who was clearly eager to talk wedding plans this morning, despite it being Christmas Day. She was pressing in on some questions that Anne felt she couldn't answer until she'd had time to learn what Grant was thinking and feeling.

Like every young girl, she had dreamed of her wedding day, but now all of those former thoughts were useless to her. This wedding had to reflect her intended, as well as the conditions under which they would be wed. Mary seemed to understand Anne's hesitant responses, and she relented. Patting Anne's hand across the table, she told her that "pearhaps the two of you need some more time ta discuss all that's taken place."

Just then Gena appeared at the table to join in. Anne was looking forward to getting to know this curious little sister of Grant's. She seemed so different from the other women in the family. Grant offered to help in the kitchen, so Anne began to inquire about Gena's school endeavors and life in general.

Gena was eager to talk about herself and her plans. Seems she had finished school and had taken a couple of different jobs in town but had never taken a liking to any of them. So she had enrolled in a nursing program at the University of Glasgow, where she lived on campus. Gena went on about her classes and her friends. Anne kept encouraging her because she was gaining so much insight into this newfound friend and soon-to-be sister.

As the table was being set around them, the girls moved over to the living room couch, where they continued their chat near the warmth of the fireplace. It didn't take long for the conversation to turn to talk of a wedding. Once again, Anne felt she had no answers to give Gena on particulars, such as where they would wed, what she would wear, what the date would be, and so on.

Soon Mr. Donaldson entered the back door, apparently coming in from an early morning bit of tinkering in the workshop. Everyone was in the home now, and the smells of sweet and savory cooking were coming from the kitchen—a perfect morning, thought Anne. Mrs. Donaldson called all to the table, and Grant beckoned to her to sit next to him on the bench seat. This time it was George Donaldson who gave the blessing.

"Our Faither in Heaven, blessed be your name above all others. We are humbly grateful ta you for this food an for this Christmas Day. We acknowledge your hand in everythin' an ask that you never stop leadin' us by that great hand. We thank you for the Christ-child who came ta save the souls of all who believe. And, of course, we thank you for the gift of new love in this household. Bless Anne an Grant as they seek your will in their plans ta marry. In Christ we pray. Amen."

Once again, Anne found herself fighting back the tears. Unlike last night, when the tears were from being overwhelmed and a bit fearful, these were feelings of joy and a sense of unconditional acceptance and love. But it was Grant who broke the silence first after the lovely prayer.

"So, Anne, we need ta know more about the traditions of American weddin's." She found that so amusing because she had been having thoughts of how to accommodate his family traditions in this wedding!

"Well," she started out, "firstly, it is traditional for the bride's family to pay for the wedding."

The frugal Mr. Donaldson couldn't resist—he nodded heartily and said, "So far, I am likin' this arrangement!"

Anne went on to explain that if there was to be a rehearsal for the families and those involved in the ceremony, that event usually took place the night before and was typically paid for by the groom's family. Anne smiled and looked at Mr. Donaldson as she spoke. This time he piped in with "Aye, but who needs practicin' for such things?"

Grant was grinning from ear to ear as he played the observer in this discussion. Anne reached over to tickle his side, but he grabbed her wrists and pulled her closer to himself before she could accomplish the task. As his strong arms enfolded her, he proceeded.

"Well, ma first order of business is ta set a date. Can we at least settle on that? And, you need ta know that I'm in a hurry!"

Anne was once again impressed with Grant's ability to lead and make his wishes known. He was fun, playful, and loving, but also exhibited a command presence and a serious but sensitive nature. It was all of this that had drawn her to him to begin with, along with the fact that he was a hopeless romantic . . . and an endless romancer.

"Surely we can do that," Anne stated with clarity. "We met in the fall, were engaged in the winter, so let's marry in the spring."

Grant jumped right on the bandwagon with, "Aye, let's get married on ma birthday—and you'll be ma present."

Anne felt her face flushing but was determined to keep up with him. "Fine, when is your birthday?" she asked.

Mrs. Donaldson chimed in that he had taken forever to be born due to his large size but entered the world on May 27, 1949.

Anne couldn't believe what she had just heard. "Did you say May 27?"

Mary Donaldson nodded affirmatively.

"Why, that's my birthday too!" exclaimed Anne.

Pushing it further, Grant chimed in, "Great. We'll be wearin' our birthday suits on our weddin' night anyway, so that seems pearfect!"

Anne could no longer hide her embarrassment. She buried her face in Grant's chest, while the rest of the family seemed to think that was a real knee-slapper.

After breakfast was eaten and the dishes cleared away, the family all moved to the living room to share the few gifts that were under the Christmas tree. Cuddling up next to Grant, Anne watched the family as they enjoyed the giving and receiving with each other. She wished she had brought more than the chocolates for the Donaldson family, but she was also secretly wishing for an opening so she could give Grant the gift she had brought specifically for him. She had stuffed the envelope for him deep into the Christmas tree branches, and when the time felt right, she walked over to pull it out and present it to him.

"Merry Christmas . . . hope you like it," she announced to Grant.

He seemed genuinely surprised and then a bit deflated as he proceeded to tell her that he'd spent his last on her ring. Anne snuggled back into his side and hugged him as she thanked him for it. "You're the best Christmas present ever," she said to him softly.

Planting a kiss on her cheek, Grant then opened the envelope and unfolded the document inside and read it. Not sure what it meant, he asked Anne to explain what he was holding in his hands. Reminding Grant that she was in training to be a money and fund manager, she informed him that she had bought him one hundred dollars worth of American stock—evenly divided between two blue-chip companies that traded on the New York Stock Exchange.

She went on to tell him that he should put the document in a safe place and forget about it, as she would be his advisor on reinvesting dividends, calls, and so on. His face lit up as he turned to his father.

"She's not only a beauty, she's ma wealth manager naw!" he said.

Mr. Donaldson shot back with, "Aye lad, you'll soon learn that they always manage your money . . . jes ask your mam!"

25

WITH gifts exchanged, it was Mrs. Donaldson who switched on the television to watch the Queen's speech. Anne watched Mr. Donaldson flash a nod to Grant, and the two of them quickly retreated to the workshop out back. Anne wasn't about to miss this, so she eagerly moved over to sit in the warm space Grant had been occupying on the couch to be closer for viewing.

She listened intently as the Queen's lilting English accent seemed to dance over every word she spoke. The Queen appeared so stately and controlled, a demeanor Anne admired greatly. In light of what had been going on in Ireland, the Queen focused her remarks on reconciliation. The whole thing seemed to strike the right chord for the times, but Anne wasn't sure how it would be received in this country. Though Anne had registered to vote as soon as she turned eighteen and was fairly informed about politics in her own country, she surely didn't understand all that was in the hearts of those in the United Kingdom—much less Ireland.

After the speech-watching, Gena sheepishly admitted to Anne that she loved doing hairdressing as a hobby. Gena asked if she could spend the rest of the morning playing with Anne's hair to see if they could find a style she might want for the wedding. That sounded great to Anne, and Mrs. Donaldson told the girls to start with washing Anne's long hair in the kitchen sink before she had to start the late-afternoon supper. Anne had brought her hair-dryer—a tool Gena was looking forward to using, since she didn't own one. Perhaps that's why Gena kept her hair short, thought Anne.

By the time Grant and his father returned to the house, Gena had washed and dried Anne's tresses and was using her old curling iron to create loose spiral curls. Grant stopped by his old bedroom to see what the two were up to and to ask Gena when she wanted him to drive her back to campus that evening.

"Right after supper, please," she responded, as she continued to concentrate on Anne's curls. Grant felt like he was intruding on girl talk, so he departed to station himself in front of the television with his father.

Within short order, both Anne and Gena emerged from the bedroom to gauge reactions from the rest of the family.

"Oh, Gena," said her mother, "you're so talented. An Anne, you look lovely."

Grant turned to see Anne's blonde locks cascading down from several silver clasps that Gena had placed asymmetrically in the hairdo. "That's it!" he stated outright.

"You like it?" Anne asked.

Grant shot back with, "Aye, it's lovely, but that's not what I meant. I meant—that's it—you're mine naw, an I am in need of your attention! Grab your coat, lass, let's take a walk before supper."

With coats donned, Grant escorted Anne out the front door. When they reached the end of the front walkway, he took her hand and turned in the opposite direction from the church and his apartment. For a split second they caught each other looking down at their entwined hands. Looking up at Grant, Anne speculated, "I think the spaces between your fingers were meant for mine." He smiled in agreement and then squeezed her hand tighter.

They walked several more blocks in silence before Grant spoke, asking Anne the inevitable question about where they would marry. Now this was something she was very clear on because she knew she'd need her mother's help. "Why, in New York, of course." That was the answer Grant was expecting but not necessarily happy about.

He protested a bit about how difficult and expensive it would be for his family to participate in a New York wedding. He raised questions about his ability to travel to the States, as well as the issue of marriage recognition in Scotland. This whole matter went to the question behind the question—that of where they would reside and citizenship.

Anne had already considered that this was going to be a complicated thing to resolve, but she reminded Grant that her father was an attorney and he could help them sort it all out. However, she pursued hard after his heart's desires. He was aware of her deference but wanted to find solutions that would make his future wife content.

Grant stopped and turned to her, opening his coat to invite her to wrap her arms around his waist for warmth. She gladly reached around him and pressed her cheek to his big chest.

Finally, she drew her head back to look up at Grant and started to pour out her heart to him.

"Grant, while I want you and your family to come to New York for the wedding, I know how much you love Scotland. It's so obviously in your blood, family, and history. So, I want you to know that I love you and that where you are, I will be also—your people will be my people. Ultimately, I know we will return from the wedding in New York to live here in Glasgow, our home."

Grant put his head on hers, held her tighter until it seemed as if his whole body enveloped hers. He was silent for a minute, and she wondered what was going through his mind and heart. He loosened his grip on her, and she thought she heard a slight crack in his voice, but perhaps she imagined that.

"Lass, you are truly a gift to me. We will marry in New York an then return ta Glasgow together. I love you, and I thank you for seein' into ma heart."

Anne looked into his eyes and felt as if she were falling into them. He was a magnet to her, and they were immediately locked in a passionate kiss right there in full public view.

26

ARRIVING back home, the couple sat down to the supper table with the family. Grant confirmed for his family that he and Anne would be married in the States but return to Glasgow to make their permanent home. His parents appeared relieved but still had several questions about dual citizenship, the potential for Anne to naturalize as a citizen, and what the status might be of any children from the marriage. Anne told them that she would rely on her father's legal advice on these matters and inform Grant in their communications leading up to the wedding. Though frankly, she was still trying to imagine telling her parents that she was engaged—much less bringing up the subject of marriage legalities.

While at the table, Mrs. Donaldson informed the couple that while they were on their walk, Pastor McGinty had phoned to ask if Grant would bring Anne with him to meet in the pastor's study at the church tomorrow at 10:00 a.m.

"Ceartainly we will," Grant answered for the two of them. Besides, he noted, perhaps the parson would have some insight into marriage legalities between the two friendly nations.

After the wonderful Christmas dinner was consumed, Grant and Anne were to take Gena back to her dormitory on campus. While Gena was gathering her things to return to school, Grant sat down at the family piano and began playing and humming bits of tunes in his head. Anne had longed to again hear him sing the song he'd written and sung in church that day she first saw him, so she asked him if he would sing it for her.

He asked her to sit on the bench with him as he played and sang. Of course, he sang it in the "old language," but when it came to the chorus, she was able to hum along. Grant seemed surprised and pleased that she joined him. The second time he came to the chorus, she hummed in harmony, and his eyes lit up. Upon conclusion, he leaned over to kiss her and then said, "Lassie, you've been keepin' secrets from me. Naw I know you can sing . . . beautifully, I might add."

Anne denied it and reminded him that he'd be the singer in the family. Her job, she pronounced, would be to figure out a way to help him pursue his dreams.

As the three piled into Grant's car, Gena reminded her brother to stop by his place so he could show Anne where he lived. That's just what they did. Driving to the back of the home to park, the three let themselves in the back door. The old home was very run-down and in serious need of repairs, but it had provided Grant with a measure of independence at a reasonable price for many years now.

He called out to Mrs. McBride, but no answer returned. He wasn't really expecting an answer, as she'd been invited to spend the holidays with a distant cousin in Edinburgh. Grant showed Anne exactly where he had sat to read her first letter to him. Climbing the narrow stairs to the small room and bath above the kitchen, she saw just how small the space was for such a big man. A rickety metal bed, a small dresser, a chair, and a round side table were just about all the room could hold. But there, leaning up against the wall, was the guitar case she recognized.

After he locked up the back door and they were walking to the car, Anne innocently made a remark about the room just needing a woman's touch. Grant stopped Anne but waved off Gena, who proceeded to the car. This time Grant had a look on his face that she'd not seen before—one of sadness. He seemed about to tell her something but then changed his mind and opened the car door for her. She wondered what he was thinking but not telling her.

The three drove to the university campus, and Anne was so very impressed. It was the beautiful gothic architecture that was so stunning, especially as the sun was setting after only coming out from the overcast for a short time in the late afternoon. Gena was nonstop chatter about this place and that, pointing at all things for Anne to see. Even after Grant parked the car and got out, Gena was still talking while he lifted her overnight bag out of the trunk.

They walked toward her all-girls dorm, and Grant stayed in the lobby to wait for Anne to return. The girls went up the stairs to Gena's room, while Gena was still carrying on! After about twenty minutes in the room, they walked back down the stairs to find Grant waiting patiently. Anne put her arms around Gena and thanked her for the hairdo, her friendship, and her hospitality. Though the two girls looked nothing alike, they felt like sisters already.

Wishing Gena a good term at school, Anne and Grant began walking toward the car when the bells of the tower that stood tall overlooking the West End of Glasgow rang out on this Christmas night. The couple slowed their pace, even finding a bench to sit on for a time, before getting too cold to remain.

Once in the car, Grant drove around campus a bit more though night was falling. They made a stop in the empty parking lot near Memorial Chapel. Getting out of the car to explore and finding the chapel door open, they walked in to see the lovely sanctuary. Engraved across the communion table in front was the university motto in Latin. Anne asked Grant if he knew what it meant.

"Naw Anne, you know I'm not an educated man and ceartainly don't know Latin."

She hadn't meant to embarrass him, but he asked her the meaning—sincerely wanting to know. "It's from scripture" she said. "It says, 'The Way, the Truth, the Life."'

Returning to the car, Grant turned the key in the ignition to get some heat going. He seemed to return to his earlier sadness, saying, "Anne, I know you see I don't have much to offer you in this life. I figure you were to a manor born, but I cannot provide what you're likely accustomed to. Are you sure you'll be happy with me here?"

Now she understood his feelings of concern. It reminded her of the feelings she'd had the night before. She felt so unable to make him feel better but reminded him, "Where you are, I will be also . . . and it will be home. And you will be all I need in this life. Besides, God will provide and perhaps, Lord willing, even prosper us."

Grant took her hand and kissed it gently. From there, he turned himself toward her and kissed her lips with an intensity she had not expected. In fact, he was gripping her shoulders with his strong hands and breathing hard. She felt her heart pounding faster as she boldly met every one of his deep kisses. He reached down to turn off the car with one hand but never left her lips in the process.

Grant then proceeded to untie the thin silk ribbon that gathered the neckline of her blouse. Within minutes his hand had moved underneath her coat, sweater, blouse, and bra strap to slip them down—baring her shoulder to his continued caresses. It was in that moment that she realized all of her mental and physical capacity to resist him had vanished.

Grant seemed to sense it too and abruptly caught himself. He stopped and sat back in the car seat, inhaling and exhaling deeply before apologizing. Having stumbled into a realization, he said, "I know naw that I can't count on you ta stop me. I'll have ta be strong for the both of us."

Pulling herself together, she agreed. "I love you so much, Grant, that my desire is to submit to you. But we've committed before God and others to wait, and we will."

Grant responded with a frustrated, "Aye, that we will."

Starting up the car again, they drove home while Anne took the opportunity to ask Grant about his relationship with his father. It led Grant to tell Anne everything he felt he must tell her anyway, so it all came out. He told her of his rebellious teen years, which turned into rejecting his father's offers of joining him in the business. Instead he had taken a factory job after school and then moved out when he turned nineteen. Grant was relieved that he was required to keep his eyes on the road, not wanting to look at Anne as he recounted his story. His early twenties had involved most nights in a pub after work, drinking heavily.

As he pulled into the driveway and turned off the car, he did look her in the eyes to tell her that those years involved what he referred to as "wild romances" bereft of any love. He held her hands as he told her that he reached the end of himself by age twenty-five.

Now the story became his testimony, and she listened intently. Grant told her of a particularly difficult day with his boss at the factory, when he had almost quit work on the spot. He instead took it out on many pints in a local pub and then planned to crawl back to his father to accept working for him. But in despair, he stopped at the family church he'd abandoned for years.

As he pulled up to the church, Pastor McGinty was just leaving for the night. With his drunken self and his beer breath, he called out to the parson, who brought Grant back into the sanctuary where they sat and talked for nearly an hour. By the end of that hour, Grant confessed his sin and his need for a savior. Pastor McGinty told Grant, "Naw you can return ta your faither, dear prodigal. Ask him for forgiveness an reconcile. He'll not turn you away, for I know the man's heart for his only son. I've heard his prayers for you, Grant."

Grant held her hands even more tightly as he pleaded with her to understand that he'd enter their marriage with a past, but that he hoped she'd walk with him into the future. Anne cupped his chin in her small hands and replied, "Oh, Grant, you are not your past—you must remember that you are forgiven and whole in the sight of God, because you are in Christ. We've all sinned and fallen short, so I am just a fellow traveler in this world. Look at my own weakness exhibited not twenty minutes ago. I want, and God wants me, to be your virginal wife, yet how readily I would have given myself to you if you had pressed me."

As he looked into her blue eyes, Grant said, "Anne, I pray ta God you will still feel that way when you know the whole story. You need ta know that seven years ago one of those rebellious nights resulted in a pregnancy, an a child I've never seen. When she told me she was pregnant, ma hard heart offered her a loveless marriage, which she rejected. She did marry another within a few months, an that man naw claims ma six-year-old son."

As his story unfolded, Anne dropped her hands to her lap and turned her face toward the car window, so he wouldn't see the pain in her eyes. She could hardly believe what she was hearing. Her mind was racing so fast she didn't even acknowledge his apologies for not having told her this before he proposed.

When finally she turned back to face him, the tears were streaming down her face. In a halting voice she said, "It is one thing to have a past, but a very different thing when the past leaves a permanent mark on your future. If this woman and your child live in this town, you are asking me not only to forgive but to forget . . . or at least pretend that it won't be a factor in our married life together. I'm not sure I can do that."

With that she turned away again, with Grant pleading, "Anne, please don't turn away from me."

Upon collecting herself, Anne entered the family home in silence, with Grant following behind her. They found Grant's parents sitting at the dining table having tea. The older couple invited the chilly younger couple to join them to warm up. As Grant poured the tea in Anne's cup, she couldn't help but wonder how much pain his parents must have gone through seven years ago. Then again, she thought, how much did they really know? However, she was still reeling and didn't feel she should bring up the matter. The two couples shared with and cared for one another for several hours that night before Grant said good night and returned to his apartment.

27

WHEN Anne awoke on Boxing Day, she dressed and wandered into the living area. The fireplace was roaring, but all she heard was some clanging of dishes in the kitchen. She peeked into the kitchen to see Mary Donaldson at work. Anne felt she'd always think of Mary in this way, holding court in her kitchen.

"Good morning!" announced Anne.

"Aye, guid mornin' ta you—George has gone off to the shop, even on this holiday, so it's jes us girls. Can I offer you some tea and toast?" Mary asked. The two sat down, and Anne ate heartily, not sure she'd see homemade bread again for months.

After several minutes of general chitchat, Mary placed her hand on Anne's hand and asked her a question that cut right to the heart. "Anne, do you really love ma son?"

The question reminded Anne of the one her father had asked, and she could feel the sting of tears again. Anne's voice cracked as she whispered in response, "Beyond all measure."

With that, Mary excused herself, handing Anne a pretty

linen hanky she pulled from her apron pocket as she stood up. In the moments Mary was gone, Anne was still trying to process what she had learned last night—and she wondered if it was the reason for Mary's question.

Within a few minutes Mary returned to the dining table with a cloth bag. "I want you ta take this home with you. As you plan the weddin', I hope you may find a way ta use it. Don't tell Grant about it, but I assure you, when he sees it, it will mean so much ta him."

Anne opened the bag and pulled out a single long piece of folded material—Donaldson tartan. Anne ran her hand over the red, blue, black, and green plaid material.

"Oh, Mrs. Donaldson—thank you. I will find a way."

Anne could hear Grant's car in the driveway, so she dashed off to put the bag in her suitcase. As she zipped it away in a hidden place, she could hear Grant coming through the front door and greeting his mother.

Anne returned to the living room, where Grant planted a kiss on her head. He then entered the kitchen to retrieve another mug for tea and returned to the table to sit down. Anne couldn't resist any longer. Standing behind the bench where Grant was sitting, she kissed him on that beautiful bald head of his! While drinking from his mug with one hand, he reached around her with his other hand and pinched her backside gently. Without missing a beat, he immediately began to recount his plan for the day. With just one full day remaining together after this, he seemed very focused this morning.

They would need to make their appointment with Pastor McGinty at 10:00 a.m. at the church, but Grant also wanted to get Anne over to see the family business, to the market, to George Square, to lunch, and to Mac's. Anne was so excited about the itinerary that she hugged Grant and thanked him, in advance, for taking her sightseeing.

"Sightseein'? No, lassie, I'm jes introducin' you ta your future home. I hope you'll someday be showin' others this proud city!"

The two grabbed their outerwear and headed out the door. But before walking out, Grant turned to kiss his mother on the head too. Backing out of the driveway onto the street, Grant asked Anne what the time was. She looked at her watch and told him it was nine o'clock. "Okay, we'll stop at the shop first." In short order they pulled up to the curb to park. Anne could see they were right in front of the quaint little shop—with many clocks on display in the window.

The shop was dark and closed for the holiday, so Grant pulled out his key to let them in. Locking the door behind them, he strode to the back while Anne was still admiring the shop contents and listening to the mixture of clock sounds. There were beautiful clocks covering the walls, standing clocks, and handsome watches resting in their glass cases. While she was still taking it all in, Mr. Donaldson emerged from the back of the shop. He barked out, "Whatcha think of the shop, Anne?" She was briefly startled and wondered to herself if she'd ever get used to his gruff ways. It was so unlike what she'd grown up with.

"Oh, Mr. Donaldson, it is beautiful—and jam-packed with amazing timepieces," she said. George waved at her to beckon her to the back of the shop, and she followed.

The back of the shop consisted of a large room that doubled as office and workbench area, as well as a small bathroom just off of the room.

"This is where we spend our time when there are no customers," announced Mr. Donaldson.

Anne noticed that Grant was sitting at the desk looking over some paperwork. The two men spent some time telling her about the history of the business. It had been passed down from Grant's deceased grandfather, who had moved his family to the city from a small family farm in the highlands. According to George Donaldson, the clan had raised sheep there for many generations—generations he claimed he could trace back to Alba. He then lightly socked Grant in the shoulder, saying, "But this boy wouldn't know how ta shear a sheep for anythin'."

Anne moved to put her hand on Grant's other shoulder, and mustering up her best Scots imitation, she said, "Aye, but he can sing the wool off an entire 'erd of 'em."

The two men simultaneously broke up laughing. When Grant finally collected himself, he said, "That was pretty guid, lass!" To which Anne responded, "Well, they do say that imitation is the highest form of flattery," covering for her secret desire to defend Grant against any ridicule, even from his father.

The couple locked up after letting themselves out the front door and then got back in the car. Anne was relieved that Grant was oblivious to her feelings about the transaction that had occurred back in the shop. As each day went by, her love for and loyalty to Grant grew stronger. She knew his father loved Grant, but she wished George wouldn't tease his son in this way. She sat quietly in the car and prayed that the Lord would intervene in the matter, for she wanted Grant to have and receive the respect of his father. Certainly Anne respected Grant, and she believed that respect would have to be the foundation for any future they might have together.

Next on their list was their meeting with Pastor McGinty. They pulled into the parking lot and jumped out to be on time. The parson was actually standing outside his office door when they walked into the church. He greeted them with gusto and ushered them into his study just off the narthex.

Asking the couple to be seated in the chairs in front of his desk, Pastor McGinty sat down at his chair across from them. Clearing his throat, he started with, "I suppose you're wonderin' why I asked for this meetin'."

He was certainly right about that, but up until last night, Anne hadn't put much thought into this meeting because she and Grant had been so caught up in each other. The pastor went on to say that he had a three-pronged purpose for the meeting.

First, he wanted to provide them with some marital advice—something Anne and Grant were eager to hear. Secondarily, he wanted to tell them that he'd written a "To whom it may concern" letter regarding their hand-fasting ceremony because it dawned on him that (in the absence of the old practice of the banns of marriage) they might need to present it to U.S. officials if they married there. This letter would explain that there had been a formal and public announcement of their engagement and intent to marry before a church in Scotland, and that there were no objections or legal barriers to the marriage.

Finally, he wanted to impress upon Grant how important it would be for him to write a letter to Mr. Ledwell to send home with Anne. It was this last matter that really had Grant's attention. He listened intently as the good reverend explained how critical it would be for Grant to declare his love for Anne and his desire for the blessing of the Ledwells on the marriage. This wasn't something Grant had considered, but the wisdom of the advice was clear to him. Anne sensed that this was weighing heavy on Grant—probably because he had less than forty-eight hours to complete this important task.

The couple spent the next hour and a half listening to the pastor's advice, answering his questions, asking him questions, and praying together. The pastor didn't avoid the subject of Grant's past and told Anne that she must pray and search her heart when determining whether or not she could live with the reality. As they departed, Pastor McGinty shook Grant's hand and gave Anne a big hug, saying, "Tell your father that the two of you have ma blessin', an he's welcome ta communicate with me about the matter." He then turned to Grant and simply said, "Honor God, an honor Anne."

Grant shook his hand, looked over at Anne, and responded to the pastor saying, "With everythin' in me, I will."

The couple spent the rest of their day in and about town enjoying lunch, window-shopping, town history, and each other. It was evident that Grant was very proud of his hometown. While Anne was glad to see him in his element, she found herself haunted by the faces of every young boy child she saw that day on the streets of Glasgow.

Their last stop was Mac's at about four in the afternoon. Grant had informed Anne that the pub was closed this day but would open about eight o'clock tonight, and he and his band mates would perform again at 8:30 p.m. Grant told her that he'd take her home after a one-hour practice session now, and they'd have dinner with his parents. He would have to leave her briefly to go to his apartment and then head back to Mac's at 7:30 p.m. for setup and a sound check, but Mr. Donaldson would drop her off in time for the performance.

Anne didn't care about the logistics. She was thrilled just to have an opportunity to hear Grant sing again!

Anne spent the time listening to Mac spin yarns while the band did what Grant called "ray-hearse-in." It was so good to see Andrew, Conor, Ryan, and Ian once again. And they, in turn, treated Anne like a princess. Anne hadn't known that Andrew and Conor were at the Christmas Eve service, so everyone knew of their engagement now. And when she heard Conor yip during practice, she recognized the same sound that had emanated from the back of the church on Christmas Eve.

After dinner back at the Donaldson home, Grant kissed Anne good-bye at the door before dashing off to his apartment. She suspected he was going to put his pen to paper for that letter to her father she would carry back to New York. Oh, how she wanted her parents to know how in love she was, though she certainly dreaded the separation from Grant. But how to tell them about his history weighed heavy on her heart. This, because she was still struggling with the matter herself.

At about eight o'clock, Mr. Donaldson drove Anne back to Mac's. Insisting on walking her into the pub, he handed her over into Mac's care before heading home to bed. Anne appreciated the personal "handling" because she just wasn't used to what she considered a bar. While "bar-hopping" had been a common Saturday-night ritual in college, she had not been one to join in, opting instead to hit the books. However, she was getting the sense that the concept of a bar in the United States and a pub in the United Kingdom were probably quite different.

Beyond that, there was the fact that far too many unattached men in these places seemed to be seeking attachment by trying to strike up a conversation or buy her a drink. Mac was there to keep them at bay. In fact, this time he sat her on a tall stool at the bar so that she would be even closer to his watchful eye.

By 8:30 sharp the band appeared on stage to much applause. Anne was in thrall every time she heard Grant's voice in solo, and she listened even more carefully to pick him out in group harmonies. She had figured out the curious fact that the two deepest voices in the group were those of Grant and Conor—the oldest and the youngest. The voices of Andrew, Ryan, and Ian were tenor, and the latter had a distinct and stylized voice, making him a great soloist. Anne was thoroughly enjoying herself and so happy to see her love enjoying himself on stage.

About halfway through the set, Andrew took over a microphone to announce a new song written by Grant, simply called "Woman." Andrew went on to say that the mates had heard the song coming on from Grant over the last month, but tonight he would sing it for the first time—dedicated to the woman he had just become engaged to.

As Grant pulled up a stool and picked up his guitar, he turned to face Anne's direction. As he did, it was Andrew who pointed to her and asked the crowd to give a hand to Grant Donaldson and his bride to be, Anne Ledwell. The crowd went wild, but as they started to hush, Anne heard a patron at the bar ask another, "He's marryin' an English?"

Forgetting all that she was hearing around her, she was totally fixated on Grant as he began to sing the beautiful love song to her—as though they were the only two in the room. And how she wished they were.

28

It was difficult for Anne to awaken to the day. However, she did awaken—and then promptly pulled the covers over her head. Though she tried, she was unable to fight back the thoughts of her visit coming to an end tomorrow and having to say good-bye to Grant. To keep herself from crying, she held her breath for a long time and then exhaled. Then she got up to collect her things and make her way to the bathroom. This morning she let the shower wash away her sadness and kept telling herself to get a grip.

By the time she had dressed, fixed her hair, and dashed on some makeup, she could hear Grant's voice in the main room of the house. She finished up quickly because he'd said he wanted to start their road trip early this morning. As she made her way to the living room, she could hear Grant talking to his mother in the kitchen, but this time it wasn't English they were using. Their voices were a bit elevated—maybe even angry—and it sounded more like the old Scottish language they were speaking. She froze in place to eavesdrop, though she couldn't really understand what they were saying—except when she heard her own name.

Not wanting to be the subject of discord, she thought she'd let her presence be known, so she appeared in the kitchen entrance. What she found was Grant comforting his mom, who had her face buried in his chest. Grant saw Anne, though his mother did not. He did not say a word, so she slowly backed away and went to stand in front of the fireplace to get warm.

Muffled sounds came from the kitchen, and then Grant came out and stood next to her. He leaned over and whispered in her ear, "Give her a minute an she'll be fine."

That minute gave him the opportunity to kiss Anne, which she eagerly received. She tried for another, but Grant seemed distracted over the matter he had been discussing with his mom.

Finally, he asked Anne if she was hungry. And she definitely was—telling Grant that breakfast was her favorite meal of all. He claimed to be a supper man himself. She tucked that bit of information away and momentarily drifted off into thoughts of how she'd need to learn more about cooking.

Finally, Mrs. Donaldson emerged from the kitchen with the teapot and cups. Without even looking up, she waved at them to come to the table. Going back into the kitchen and emerging with some amazing sweet rolls, Mary Donaldson had collected herself and was ready to join in the morning conversation. The three ate their fill and talked about today's adventure.

Grant wanted to take Anne on a trip to see more of his beloved Scotland. He gave her three options. He could take her to see the beauty of the northland in Inverness, take her on a trip to see important historic sites from Stirling to Arbroath, or take her to spend their day in the enchanting city of Edinburgh, visiting castles, museums, and galleries.

"Oh, Grant, I can't choose—tell me you'll one day take me to see all of it!" she pleaded.

Smiling so that his dimples appeared, he put his arm around her and said, "Your wish is ma command, lass—but we have only this day. I'd like you to know more of our history and see the shore, so let's head to Arbroath. It's only about two hours, but we'll make many stops. I don't want to hurry, for this day must last." Surely, Grant was feeling the same dread of parting that Anne had awoken to this morning.

With that, Mrs. Donaldson disappeared into the kitchen and returned with a basket of food she'd put together for their lunch. Anne marveled at how practical and frugal Mary was—especially in light of the fact that her own mother would have been mapping out all the dining establishments where they could stop for breakfast, lunch, *and* dinner! The two collected their coats, scarves, hats, and even gloves, for it would be a cold winter adventure, especially on the shores of the North Sea.

As they pulled out of the driveway, Anne was not only excited about the things she would learn and see on this outing but also thrilled at the prospect of having Grant all to herself. After a few minutes of silence as she let Grant concentrate on his route, she broke in with another round of gushing praise for the music and the special song the night before. He smiled and patted her hand with his free hand but didn't say a word. Anne was beginning to wonder if the discussion with his mother this morning was weighing heavy on him, even now.

As more silence passed, she quietly opened with, "Do you want to talk about it?"

This time he briefly looked at her without any expression on his face before looking back at the road. Finally, his broad shoulders rose up and then down with a big sigh, and he began to pour it out. Grant explained that his mother was none too happy about this day trip they were taking. She felt it might not reflect well on Anne to be unchaperoned with him all day. She had also expressed some old fears about his having known the pleasures of a woman's arms.

Anne was getting the message loud and clear and now understood what was bothering Grant. She finished his thought for him when she said, "You're hurt because she doesn't trust you."

Grant affirmed that conclusion and went on to say that his mother had lectured him about his judgment for taking the trip, and on keeping his pants zipped.

That comment pinned Anne back in her chair, unable to look at him due to her own embarrassment. He looked over at her and began laughing.

"What's so funny?" she asked while still looking straight ahead.

"Ah, lass, you are so tender an naïve. I'm thinkin' such a conversation would never happen between you an your parent! That's probably the Brit in you—so proper an upright. Well, you need ta know that we Scots are a bit more earthy."

Anne didn't know if he was making an accurate assessment or insulting her.

Grant went on, "Anne, I am hurt that she didn't trust me—an she may even be right about the trip—but I'm makin' the call for us. Besides, what really matters ta me is that you trust me."

After what seemed like an eternity, Anne turned to look out the passenger window, while responding that she had put her trust in him.

After a few more quiet moments, Anne had more questions.

"So what did you tell your mother? And by the way, what was that language you spoke?"

Grant explained that he had told his mother, "I love Anne too much ta take advantage of her, I respect her faither too much ta do that, and I fear God too much ta do that."

"You see, Anne," he continued, "although I don't know that I deserve you, I would have ma virgin bride on our weddin' night."

There wasn't much more Anne wanted to know, as she was already uncomfortable hearing that he and his mother had had a conversation of this nature. Anne was beginning to wonder if perhaps Grant had made an accurate assessment about her being a bit priggish.

Later, as they approached Stirling Castle, Grant piped up with "Scots braid, darlin'–the family still speaks it at home from time ta time."

While she realized he was answering her earlier question, Anne was busy marveling at what she saw ahead of her in the distance. She was awestruck by the beautiful fortress on the crag. As Grant drove to the site, parked the car, and pulled on the hand brake, he finished his thought. "'Cause that's what we are—Scots—an proud of it. An this place, sweet Anne, is like a pilgrimage ta sacred ground for the likes of me!"

With that, he sprang from the car while she was still looking up at the magnificent edifice in front of her. She was, however, so glad to see his spirits lifted as they walked up the hill. With her arms wrapped around one of his, she asked him to speak Scots to her. Grant spoke loud enough for others within earshot to hear–"Ma laddie, herken to the advisins o' yer faither, an' dinna mislippen the biddens o' yer mither, for they'll e'en be like a bonnie croon on the heid o' ye."

Anne squealed with delight and then promptly asked him what he'd said.

"I was jes quotin' some scripture for you, lass—wise words from King Solomon they be."

This was going to be a wonderful day!

Touring the beautiful castle, Anne was enchanted by the fact that she was walking through chambers once occupied by Mary, Queen of Scots. She lingered quite a while before the dramatic tapestry of the fence-encircled unicorn, as Grant explained that the unicorn was the symbol of Scotland. He went on to explain that it was said that only a virgin could tame the heart of the mythical beast.

By early afternoon the two were making their way to Arbroath on the North Sea. They had concluded it might be a good place to eat the lunch that Mrs. Donaldson had packed for them. Upon arrival in the small town, they ate some of the food from the basket while trying to keep warm in the car but saved the rest as they were eager to spend some time in the old abbey.

Grant told Anne about the historic Declaration of Arbroath, believed to have been written at the abbey which was now just ruins. However, they did find the sacristy to be intact, and as they passed through its large door, Grant immediately took to the outstanding acoustics in the small room.

"Anyone could sound guid in this room!" Grant said in a somewhat hushed voice, which still rang clearly around the perfect structure. He then began to hum what sounded like Gregorian chant with that beautiful voice of his. Anne just marveled at the deep and rich sound.

"I didn't think you could sound any better—it's amazing!" she told him.

With that, he pulled her close in front of him. Looking down at her, he wondered out loud if he might be able to hear their kiss.

"Let's find out right now," Anne whispered as she stood on her toes to reach his mouth.

Continuing the tour, Anne learned that the historic declaration was sent to the pope in hopes that he would recognize the rights of the Scots to choose their king. As they walked the peaceful grounds, Grant explained to her that from childhood he and all Scottish children were taught of this declaration—and to yearn for liberty.

After they'd driven to the waterfront, the chill wind off the North Sea kept them from eating the rest of their lunch anywhere but in the car, but afterward Anne pleaded with Grant to at least take a few minutes to walk along the harbor. Donning hats and scarves again, they headed toward the small sandy area of the harbor inlet. The gray ocean horizon seemed endless before them. While walking down the concrete steps to the beach, Grant pointed to the signal tower nearby and explained to her that the building communicated with the four men stationed at the lighthouse just over ten miles out to sea. "Too bad it's such a gray day. You'll jes have ta take ma word for it—they're out there!"

They were holding each other tightly for warmth as well as for love, but Anne stopped for a second to look down. Seeing something shiny in a mess of seaweed and debris, she reached down to fish through it but quickly recoiled when she felt a sharp pain. Looking down at her hand, she realized she had a small, superficial cut across the palm that was bleeding just a bit.

Grant reached for her small hand to examine the damage. "Oh dear, let's wash it off in the sea," he advised. But before they reached the edge of the water, he pulled out the small pocketknife on his keychain. With a rapid strike of the blade against his own palm, he pressed his hand against her injury and then plunged their clasped hands into the frigid salt water. As he brought their hands back out of the water, he reminded her that this wasn't the first time the blood of a Scot and that of a Brit had mingled on Scottish shores. Then removing his scarf from around his neck, he bound her small wound with it, and they trudged back to the car arm in arm.

With the car started, the heat was beginning to warm things up when Grant turned to kiss Anne, which added to their warmth. Then she asked him why he had cut his own hand on the beach. He held her tightly to himself and whispered, "When you return home tomorrow, an for the next few days, we'll both feel the reminder of this brief pain. But, it's ma prayer that your heart will heal as quickly from the pain I brought ta you over ma past. I don't want ta lose you for this or any reason."

Anne felt the pain in her heart much more than the cut on her hand. As she uncovered her hand to look at the small wound, she looked up at Grant and in a whispered voice said, "But this pain is only temporary."

This time it was Grant who turned his face to look out the window.

The two traipsed all over Stirling, Dundee, Arbroath, and Glenrothes before returning home to Glasgow that evening for a late supper. All told, about two hundred miles, but they had taken it slow so as to savor every minute they had together. Anne loved every moment of her history lessons, the beauty of the land, and her pride in wearing Grant like a prize all day. Grant loved every moment of telling his history, the beauty of Anne, and the surety he felt that every man who had seen them together would consider him the fortunate one.

As they parted that night, Grant promised the letter for her father would be ready in the morning when he returned to take her to the airport. He gently pushed her blonde hair away from her face with his hand and kissed her good night. As she started to pull away, he held onto her tighter, as if it might help him gauge the warmth of her devotion for him. When he did finally release her, he reminded her that their birthday—their wedding day—was just five months away from this very day.

29

ANNE packed her last item of clothing and locked the suitcase. Finishing up in the bathroom, she placed on the counter the pretty silver hair clasps that Gena had used in her hair just a few days earlier. She brought her belongings into the living room, where Mr. Donaldson was first to say good-bye before leaving for the shop. Anne thanked him for his invitation and his hospitality, and he thanked her for coming to the family home.

Mr. Donaldson then picked up her lowered chin, much like Grant had done so many times, and said, "I will see that this clan is in New York on May 27 for this weddin', Anne. It will be Grant's happiest day, an we will be there ta share in it."

She reached up to hug his neck, and he picked her up off the ground—much like Grant had done so many times.

Within minutes after George's departure out the back door, Grant walked in the front door. Hardly able to look at Anne, he asked if she was ready.

"I suppose so," she responded with a sigh.

Mary Donaldson emerged from the kitchen, drying her hands on her apron and then holding out her arms to embrace Anne. That was just too much for the two of them, and tears started to flow as they said their good-byes. There was no doubt the two women had bonded during their few days together.

As Grant was picking up Anne's suitcase to carry it to the car, Mary whispered in Anne's ear, "I'll make his weddin' suit by ma own hand. He'll be the most handsome sight when you see him again on that bonnie spring day in May!"

The fog was thick on the drive to Edinburgh airport. It reflected Grant's mood—heavy and quiet. Anne didn't talk much either for fear of more tears. However, Grant pulled the envelope for her father out of his coat pocket and handed it to her, asking her directly, "What if he says no?" Anne assured him that such a thing was unlikely once her parents knew how much they loved each other. She also reminded him that she was of age and could certainly make her own decisions.

He smiled but admitted to her that he felt like he was losing her again, just as he'd felt back in September.

"No," she assured him. "We will write regularly, and I will call if necessary. I will see to the many details on my end, so that all you must do is get to the church on time on your birthday. I will send forth invitations to your family, and some extras to you for distribution to others here as you see fit. I realize there may not be a big contingent from Scotland at a New York wedding, but you're the only required attendee." Her planning and execution skills were kicking in.

But what Grant most adored was the self-assuredness exhibited by such a young girl.

"I love you, Anne—an I'll be at the church if I have to swim the Atlantic."

As they parked the car and he carried her bag into the airport for check-in, he couldn't seem to rid himself of the feeling of their being torn apart at the seam by which they had stitched themselves together during this visit. The truth was that he was feeling absolute panic inside—panic that his past might be insurmountable and that he'd never see her again.

Grant stayed with her at the gate until the boarding call and would then drive back to work at the shop until closing time. All the hand-holding, thank-yous, kisses, and reflections on their time together were drawing to an end, and the sadness they felt was palpable. As they stood to say good-bye, Grant kissed her waiting lips one last time. He seemed to tear up a bit as he quietly said, "Ma heart is breaking, lass. Go naw—an don't look back."

Anne did just that, so he never saw her crying as she walked away.

The tears in her eyes made it impossible to see the ring on her finger as she tried to look at it. She turned her hand palm up, but the tears also made it hard to see the small cut from yesterday's trip to the coast. It was a good thing she was in the lavatory on the plane where there was plenty of tissue and no one could hear her crying.

The flight attendant had seen Anne's tears when she boarded in Edinburgh and just before takeoff had asked Anne if she wanted to move to a seat in the rear with no seatmate. That was so kind of her, thought Anne, who had held it together for most of the trip. But now, with last call having been made and touchdown in New York about thirty minutes away on this last flight, she found herself breaking down again. Trying to collect herself, she splashed cold water on her face and dove into her handbag to find some lip gloss and powder to repair the damage.

As Anne had arranged, her parents were waiting at the baggage claim area. They were a sight for literal sore eyes. Her pace picked up once she spotted them, and she practically fell into their arms. After the greeting, Ken Ledwell was quick to identify her bag and pull it off the carousel. The three immediately went out to hail a cab home—but not before Ruth Ledwell spotted the engagement ring on Anne's left hand.

30

WHAT Ruth had seen she kept to herself until they arrived at home. But as soon as the front door of the apartment was closed and locked for the night, she confronted Anne.

"By what I see on your hand, it appears you have returned with some news that perhaps you'd like to share with us?" Ruth posited.

Anne reflexively raised her hand to her face, as if drawing strength from it to speak. Conscious now of what she must do, she held out her hand to her parents to show them the pretty little diamond.

"Well," said her father, "it appears that you got your question answered over there. How about we go to the living room and you tell us what you learned."

Anne still hadn't taken her handbag off her shoulder as she led the way into the living room. Pulling Grant's letter from the purse, she handed it to her father. She announced to him that she'd brought this letter from Grant as instructed when he'd taken her to the airport this morning. Furthermore, she told her parents, she had resisted reading it because she wanted her father to read it to her.

Being an attorney, her father indicated that if this was private communication, he'd first read it and then determine if it was to be shared.

That was fair enough, thought Anne, but she wanted so badly to know its contents and could hardly wait for a reading of the letter.

But before he could even open it, she began spilling over with all that had happened to her, practically tripping over her words.

"Oh, Daddy, he's the most wonderful man . . . besides you, of course. When he picked me up at the airport, he professed undying love, and I knew I felt the same. Grant proposed to me that same night—Christmas Eve—right there at the dinner table with his whole family present. He hadn't told anyone, and the surprise brought everyone together. That night at church there was a . . . well, a sort of engagement announcement by Pastor McGinty, but I'll tell you more about that later. Grant has only been a Christian for about four years, so there are things in his past he's had to reconcile, but the few days we had together were so amazing."

Ken and Ruth hadn't even sat down, but they did now.

31

ANNE just made it to her desk at the office by 8:00 a.m. the next day. Of course, Nick was on vacation, but she had lots of catching up to do. She just hoped she could keep her mind on her work . . . and stop staring at her engagement ring. She did catch up, and she did make it through the day, but not without co-workers noticing either her ring or her glowing countenance. There would be no keeping the news of her engagement a secret from her boss upon his return in the New Year, and undoubtedly it would be his executive assistant who would be the one to tell him.

That night at the dinner table, the engagement conversation continued. But best of all, Anne's father had decided he would read Grant's letter to her and her mother. In his steady and articulate voice he began reading.

Mr. Ledwell,

First let me thank you for sending Anne to Scotland for Christmas. The entire family has embraced her wonderful spirit. And I readily and eagerly admit to being in love with your daughter.

By now you may know that I proposed marriage to her on Christmas Eve, and she has accepted. However, I do not want to presume your blessing upon the marriage, so I write to formally ask that I may take her to wife.

We have discussed our hopes to marry as soon as possible, choosing our mutual birthday of May 27 of the coming year. Anne has expressed her desire to wed in New York, and then it would be my intent to bring her back to Glasgow to make our home and life together here. And though I am not certain that I am deserving of your daughter, please know that I will cherish and protect her always.

I anxiously await your response to this letter but leave all things in God's hands.

Respectfully,

Grant C. Donaldson

Anne was hanging on every word that her father read aloud. Her heart soared as she could literally hear Grant's words in his accent and intonation. How simple and straightforward it was. She was glad she wasn't the one to have to write such a letter for she felt she'd clutter it up so.

When her father finished reading, he refolded the letter and set it down before him. Looking over at Ruth, and then back at Anne, he finally spoke.

"I would like to know if you have really thought through what lies ahead of you if you choose this course. For example, what do you really know of Grant's family, his means, his past, and the potential to never live in this country again?" he asked her.

Though she wanted to blurt out so many things, she realized she would have to be measured and thoughtful in this response. Collecting herself by folding her hands in front of her she began.

"Daddy, I love him, his parents, and his siblings. They welcomed me like family even before they knew I might be. Second, both Grant and I have eyes wide open on the matter of finances. We recognize that we will struggle, at least initially—and perhaps for a lifetime. However, I would ask you to think back to your first years of marriage and how little you two had beyond your love for one another. That's what Grant and I have. And, by God's grace, you two came to Christ after you were married, but Grant and I will have the benefit of starting our union in Christ.

"Finally, you know that I love this country, and I realize that it will be very difficult to leave her to accept another national identity. But once again, I would remind you that scripture tells us this world is not our home, we are just passing through. And I have pledged myself to Grant, not to a location."

By the time she finished her last word, she was already feeling as though someone else had put them in her mouth. Furthermore, she had gotten through the whole dissertation without crying, or mentioning her own hesitations about Grant's past.

Her father looked over at Ruth, who was crying, and he took her hand in his. Looking back at Anne, he simply replied, "Yes, I understand. Then I suppose you and your mother have some wedding plans to make, and the time you have is short."

32

OVER the next week, Anne continued to ponder the things Pastor McGinty had said to her and Grant when they visited his office. To be sure, she loved Grant, but it was McGinty's question of whether or not she could live with (and perhaps even share in) the consequences of his past that kept coming back to her mind.

That following Sunday when she and her parents attended church, the pastor spoke about moving past forgiveness to living whole. It was convicting to Anne to think that Grant was living whole while she still struggled internally with the specter of another woman and his child. The previous night she had tossed and turned in bed all night with the feeling of unease. She awoke asking herself what any young girl might ask—are there no other fish in the sea? Do I need this complication in my future? But even those questions felt like the wrong questions, for she already knew she would always love him—whether they were together or not.

As the sermon concluded, the pastor gave an altar call but also invited anyone who needed prayer to come forward. Without hesitation, she rose from her seat and walked down the aisle. As she did, she noticed a man who looked to be in his fifties or so heading in the same direction. The pastor gave the benediction and dismissed the congregation then turned to the gentleman to shake his hand. Resigned to waiting her turn, Anne felt an arm around her shoulder. Looking to her left, she recognized the pastor's wife, who pulled her aside and quietly asked, "How can I pray for you, Anne?"

The tears sprang to her eyes as she revealed her dilemma to the woman.

At the end of her story, the gracious lady took Anne by the hand and said, "Dear girl, I don't presume to know more than Grant's pastor, but it seems to me that he poses the wrong question. It isn't a matter of determining whether or not you can live with Grant, but whether or not you can live without him. Let me pray that the Lord will reveal that answer and His will to you."

The two sat in a nearby pew as the older woman prayed over Anne.

As she walked out of the church and into the below-freezing temperature, Anne felt the cold but also the warmth of the sun that shone on her face. Suddenly and with great clarity, she knew what she must do. Returning home after lunch that day, she sat down at her small desk and began to write.

Dear Grant,

How I wish I could tell you in person what I'm about to say here in this letter.

I know that you have sensed my internal struggle with the revelation of your past. I want you to know that it was not you I doubted. Instead, it was my doubts about whether I could bear the burden of the consequences with you. After much prayer, the Spirit of God has shown me my brooding over a selfish claim to my own rights in all this. And more importantly, the God we both serve has assured me in His Word that "love bears all things, believes all things, hopes all things, and endures all things."

Forgive me my own weakness, and know that I am fully devoted to you and can't live without you. I long to spend my life with you, come what may.

Forever yours,

Anne

33

ANNE'S father never told her of his response to Grant, so she thought it best to wait to hear from Grant first to know that he had received it. She also wanted to know that he had received her letter. But it would be another two weeks before Grant's letter finally arrived in the mail.

My love,

Last week I received a telegram from your father. It read simply, "Yes. We look forward to the joy of May 27." Then your tender letter arrived today—a response for which I am, and will be, eternally grateful.

My heart and mind are so relieved, and I can rest in the assurance that you will soon be my wife. While I look forward to the wedding, you know that I am most eager to bring you home where I can linger in your embrace every night.

The family is happy too, and there are plans being made on this end as well. It will not be easy, but we will have as many family and friends at the wedding as possible. Even my bandmates dream of going to New York with me!

Things at the shop are going better now that my mind is at ease for us. I trust your job is going well, but tell me more about your plans on that front, given our wedding day. Please let me know if there are things I need to do on this end. I've never had a wedding before, so I feel I know nothing.

I can't wait to see you next, when you will be walking toward me instead of away.

All my love,

Grant

To Anne, Grant's letters were like works of art. She saved them all and read them often. Meanwhile, each new day brought decision points on the wedding—a wedding she was now eager to plan. It was to be held in Christ Chapel in the Riverside Church down the street from the apartment. While this wasn't their church home, Anne loved the classic architecture of the church on the Hudson River, the close proximity to the apartment, and the chapel's eleventh-century Romanesque replica of the nave of a fortress church in France. It seated about a hundred and twenty, and there was a separate space for a simple reception afterward. Anne knew it would be hard for those from the land of castles and cathedrals to be much impressed with the newer buildings in the United States, but this was a pretty venue.

The wedding would take place at high noon, followed by a simple lunch, cake, and punch. And then there was the matter of the music, her dress, and how she would incorporate the Donaldson tartan into the event. She also knew she wanted to use the braided cord from her hand-fasting ceremony somehow. There were so many details for her to consider, though at least her sisters had agreed to be in the wedding party. In fact, it was in the phone call to her eldest sister that the family learned that Clara was pregnant again! Meanwhile Anne's father was still researching the legal nuances of travel, residency, citizenship, and marriage to her handsome Scotsman.

She had faced the issue of telling Nick about her intent to marry in May and then to leave the country with her husband. He was very happy for her but was brutally honest about the fact that she was effectively tendering her resignation. She asked if she might continue working until May 5, and he had agreed. However, he told her that his plans to send her to a two-week training class that would have led to a certification would have to be cancelled. She understood but had no intention of giving up her hope of someday being in the money management game. At this point, she just didn't know what that might look like, given her future in Scotland.

Her letters to Grant became increasingly detailed in terms of information about the wedding, without giving away the secret surprises she had planned.

My precious one,

My days are filled with work, but my evenings, weekends, and head are filled with wedding plans! With March fast approaching, there are many details I must attend to. Through it all, my hopes and dreams are occupied by thoughts of you.

Expect a letter from my father explaining what you will need to accomplish through the British Consulate here in New York to obtain permission for us to be legally married here. It does appear that I can maintain my U.S. citizenship (unless

I renounce, which I don't want to do) while still naturalizing to Scotland. That will take some time after I am in Glasgow, which may affect my ability to find work there for the first year. However, given the high rate of unemployment in Scotland, I rather expected that to be a struggle anyway. Meanwhile, I will continue to hold my job here until May 5. I am saving as much money as I can to bring to the household when we are married.

My parents have heard your desire to immediately return to Scotland after the wedding, though they are saddened by thoughts of my departure. Since the wedding is on a Saturday, they are asking if they might send us to a nice hotel in the City for that night as well as Sunday night. If we return to the apartment on Monday morning, we can pack up our things and have a last meal with them, and then they will take us to the airport for our overnight flight. It's a wedding gift to us that they would pay for our brief honeymoon in New York. I hope we never leave the room for the entire time we have it!

I will be sending invitations out soon to our friends and family. Please let me know your list with addresses—beyond your immediate family, that is. We are also anxious to know who will be coming and when you will arrive! Be advised that it is tradition that the bride does not see the groom on the day of the wedding, until she walks down the aisle. I can't wait to lay eyes on you again.

With all my love,

Anne

P.S. I did ask my father if he wanted to officiate the wedding. However, he prefers to accompany me down the aisle and give me over to you, leaving the officiating to a dear friend of his instead. Also, we will have no need to memorize vows or lines, but you will have to kiss me in front of all those witnesses!

34

As Easter approached, Anne was beyond happy to learn that Mr. and Mrs. Donaldson would be in attendance at the wedding, and they would bring Gena, who had agreed to be a bridesmaid. However, Anne was disappointed that the Byrnes could not come, due to Keith's job. As the plans and information continued to be transmitted through letters, Grant passed along the wonderful news that all but one of his bandmates would be able to attend as well. Andrew, Ian, and Conor would make up the groom's party, with Conor taking up the role of best man. Anne knew that Grant had a special place in his heart for this youngest of the band—ten years his junior. Only later would she learn that it was Grant who had led the teenaged Conor to Christ, not long after Grant had himself become a believer.

The days contained more daylight and warmth as spring arrived. Anne was still busy at work but spending her weekends selecting bridesmaid gifts, her dress and shoes, and flowers, music, and food for the wedding. One of her big tasks over the holiday weekend would be to pick up the silver wedding band she had chosen to give Grant. It wasn't expensive, for this she would have to pay for out of her own funds. Collecting it from a store near her office on her way home on Good Friday, she placed it deep inside her purse and clutched the bag tightly all the way home.

Though all this preparation was great fun, she occasionally found herself crying herself to sleep for missing Grant so much. She knew it was only a matter of time until she would see him again, yet it still felt like a rending to be apart. She ever lived to receive and read his letters.

My dear lass,

I hope this letter arrives by Easter—such an amazing holiday in the life of our church. Conor, Andrew, and I will be singing with the choir that Sunday! I wish you and your family a blessed Easter there in New York.

We are now in the season of our marriage, and it won't be long until I can hold you in my arms again. I have followed all instructions, and hope I'm not forgetting to do something with regards to this wedding. It is a good thing I have Conor as my best man, for he is a good organizer and doesn't forget a thing.

I think Gena was happy about your decision to let the ladies wear any dress of their own choosing. I know my mother was happy because she is busy making Gena's dress—in addition to my wedding suit, and even those of the men taking part. She is relieved, however, not to have to worry about my father since he still fits into his formal wear!

Can you tell me the name of the parson sw who will be performing this wedding? Is there some payment I should be making to him for his services? Also, you should know that we are all flying to New York on the same plane, though only you and I will be returning on that Monday following the wedding. This side of the world will arrive late night of the wedding eve, so there will be no time for rehearsal. But my family and friends do hope your family and friends will join them for a dinner the night after the wedding—Sunday. My father invites all and would like to know of a good restaurant your father would recommend for this purpose.

Beloved, I look at your picture every day, but nothing can compare to the feel of you.

Always,

Grant

35

On Friday, May 5, Anne was surprised by her co-workers with a simple potluck at the office, and her boss rose to speak kind words of her service to the company. She felt a bit guilty, for her tenure there had been just seven months. She was glad, however, to see that Joey and Missy joined in the gathering to congratulate her. Nick was very complimentary of her work, indicating that he thought she had great potential in the world of high finance, and encouraged her to continue her education and training when she moved to "the realm," as he called it.

That actually made it sound so otherworldly. She didn't think of modern-day Scotland in that way, and it made her wish that Grant were right there in the room to answer her questions from his perspective. Her own perspective of her future home was built on an English foundation and understanding. Unaware of her lens and filter, she had seen Scotland as a proud but poorer "second sister." Though she didn't think of her future husband as a political animal, she did presume that all Scots had an opinion about their nation and how she should be viewed. Anne determined that she would make a point to learn of his.

Finishing her last assignments involved in orienting her replacement, Anne made a final report to Nick in his office. As her kind boss walked her down to the foyer where she had first presented herself for an interview, her co-workers waved to her across desks, and some even gave her hugs. Nick shook her hand in the lobby, assuring her that he and his wife would be at the wedding, and then handed her an envelope. She wasn't sure what that was but placed it carefully in her purse and said good-bye quickly, as she needed to catch her bus. On the way home she would have a chance to read the contents of the envelope.

How thoughtful, she later reflected to herself, for Nick to have written such a lovely letter of recommendation on company letterhead. She wasn't quite sure it would carry much weight in Glasgow, but she was glad to have it.

At dinner that night she told her parents about the events of her last day and that Nick had written her a recommendation. Her father encouraged Anne to place it among her important personal papers and documents that she would carry with her to Scotland after the wedding.

The conversation moved on to some disagreements Anne and her mother had over wedding details. While the two women had been largely in sync on the plans, there was some argument brewing over Anne's choice not to wear a veil or any headpiece with her dress. She had selected a beautiful but simple dress of lace over a simple, white, formfitting lining. It was Anne's taste for simple elegance, coupled with her desire to bring a Celtic influence to the wedding, that brought her to the "no veil" decision.

She had reminded her mother that it was not uncommon for a Celtic bride to wear just a simple circlet made of flowers or metal. What she really wanted was pair of silver metal hair clasps so that she might replicate what Gena had done with her hair during the Christmas visit. Ruth was not convinced, but this time Ken Ledwell decided to wade into unknown territory, saying, "Mother, this is her wedding, so let it be."

It was now just three weeks to the wedding and almost all details had been attended to. Her sisters would arrive several days before the wedding. And despite the fact that half the wedding party would be unavailable to practice, when Clara and Victoria arrived they would walk down to the church to work with the wedding coordinator on timing.

Additionally, one of the final items that Anne was waiting on was something she was expecting to arrive with her beloved aunt. Ruth had two sisters, but only Anne's Aunt Delores and her husband would be coming to the wedding. This was the doting aunt of the family, and in many ways the only person who could tame Anne's mother, for Delores was the older and bossier sister. Anne was looking forward to having her Aunt Delores in her corner on every matter leading up to the wedding!

On her way to her last day at work today, Anne had sent what she knew would be the final letter she could write to Grant before they were married. But across the Atlantic, it was going to be Grant who had the last word as he sat down to write a letter to Anne on Saturday, May 13. He knew he was cutting it close but hoped it would arrive in her hands just before the wedding.

It did, and on Thursday, May 25, Anne secreted herself away in a small side room of the church as the women of the family chatted with the wedding coordinator. She knew she was acting like a guilty schoolgirl who had hidden from authority so as not to be caught for her bad deeds. But it wasn't guilt she felt—she felt more like a hungry animal that carries its food off into the woods to devour it without interruption or concern. She was so hungry for Grant that her hands shook as she opened the letter.

My Forever Love,

This is the last letter I can write with any hope of your receipt before our wedding. It's now just two weeks before we will be united in marriage before God and witnesses. Then we will be free to share our love—and for a lifetime thereafter.

I grow so impatient in these last days. So much so that I'm almost afraid to be around others for fear I might snap at them. Of course, it's not them, but my drive to be done with this waiting period. It's as though my urges for you are like pounding drums growing louder with each passing day. I should be grateful that we have been apart during these months, lest I might break my commitment not to take you to myself. The Lord must have known what was best between us, for I am weak, but it is He who is able to keep covenants.

I will see you soon, but the greater purpose of this letter is to thank you for your willingness to take me as your husband. I am undeserving of you, but God has seen fit to honour me with you anyway. For that I am grateful, and I hope to never take for granted the gift I am about to receive in you.

Yours completely,

Grant

With tears streaming down her cheeks, Anne felt as though her heart would burst open with the flood of emotion that was now overwhelming her. She'd never be able to cover up the tracks of tears before someone found her in this side room. Trying hard to keep from crying out, she instead groaned deep inside with the pain of separation from the only man she'd ever love. She whispered to herself, "Just forty-eight more hours."

36

MAY 27 had finally come, and at exactly 11:50 a.m. the beautiful and powerful strains of Celtic pipes and string orchestra played out from the rear of the chapel as guests and family were arriving at Riverside Church on a sunny 75-degree day. The majestic but sweet song being played was unknown to most sitting in the chapel, but it signaled to attendees a somewhat nontraditional wedding.

Waiting in the wings was the wedding party, anxious to make their entry at noon. However, in the chapel most of the guests were enjoying being directed to their seats by three very handsome young men in crisp, white, open shirts, gray jackets, and matching gray kilts with black belts. The silver thistle pin on the apron of each kilt was the only flashy sign upon them, if one discounted the fact that it was flashy enough to see men in skirts at an American wedding!

Behind the side door just off the front of the chapel, Grant waited with Pastor Edwards, who would officiate the wedding. As the musicians played, Grant asked the pastor if he would mind opening the door just a crack so that he could hear the music coming from the back of the church. He let it wash over him, and suddenly all the nervousness he felt disappeared.

He looked at the chaplain and whispered, "She's chosen this beautiful music with me an ma family in mind. That's ma Anne, always considerin' others."

Pastor Edwards leaned Grant's way and whispered back, "Don't ever take her kindness for granted. And don't take advantage of it either. Love her for this trait, Grant, and you'll be a happily married man all your days."

Grant smiled at the pastor in acknowledgement.

At 11:55 a.m., with the seating of the mothers, things got a bit flashier. Andrew took Ruth Ledwell by the arm and seated her at the front pew on the left side of the aisle. As she took her seat, Andrew kissed her hand before releasing it. She looked radiant in a deep-purple two-piece dress with matching heels. Next up was Ian leading Mary Donaldson in her mauve dress to the front as the music was coming to a conclusion. Following proudly behind them was George Donaldson in full Scottish dress—looking all the Highland's son that he was, from his clan tartan kilt to his black leather sporran. Ian then kissed Mary's hand as she was seated. It was clear to all in attendance that when the Donaldson entourage went to see their fair son's wedding, they would do it up in style.

At noon the musicians began the processional song with loud bagpipe swells of "Faith of our Fathers." And with the first strain, Pastor Edwards and Grant presented front and center after emerging from their side room. The entry of the groom drew an almost audible response. At over six feet tall with his strong legs firmly set in a wide stance, Grant towered over the rest of the wedding party. He wore a beautiful black formal jacket with large, square, pewter-colored metal adornment, a black shirt and tie, a black plain-front kilt that sported a silver sword pin on the apron, a black belt with silver buckle, his ghillie brogues with clan tartan flashes on traditional black hose, and completed the outfit with an ornamental dirk.

But most impressive of all was the Donaldson plaid hanging over the back of his right shoulder, held there by a large pewter shield brooch. He was bigger than life and without a doubt the most impressive figure in the room.

At the same time that Grant appeared at the altar, the wedding coordinator was waving Ian and Gena on to be the first attendants to enter into the chapel. Though each bridesmaid had been asked to select a dress of her own choosing, Anne had given simple instructions that they be knee-length and of a single solid color.

Mrs. Donaldson had created a lovely sky-blue empire-waist dress for Gena, and her short auburn hair was coiffed to perfection. By the time Ian had deposited Gena in the front and moved to stand a few feet from Grant, the next couple was on their way down the aisle.

This time it was Anne's middle sister, Victoria. She was wearing a pink sheath dress and had her arm wrapped around the arm of Andrew. As Andrew released Victoria and took his place next to Ian, the two young men jabbed each other playfully. The more formal Ledwell family members were absolutely charmed by the very relaxed Scottish crew.

Last up the aisle was Anne's eldest sister, Clara Ledwell Johnston. Dressed in a two-piece jewel-tone green dress built for her condition of maternity, she was escorted to the front by Conor. After placing her in the appropriate spot, Conor positioned himself at Grant's left side. Grant looked confident and pleased as he surveyed the three trusted friends by his side.

There came a flourish from the musicians as they prepared for the final, elevated, and louder verse of the stately hymn, for the time had come for Anne and her father to walk the aisle. They linked arms, and Ken Ledwell leaned slightly toward Anne to ask, "Are you absolutely sure about this?"

Anne flashed her pearly smile his way, saying, "Daddy, I've never been so sure of anything in my life—or so happy."

From the moment Anne appeared in the doorway of the chapel with her father, Grant was transfixed by her natural beauty. Her white, floor-length, lace-covered gown had a small train that swept the floor behind her. Her blonde hair flowed down her back and was pulled slightly up and back from her face with two large silver clasps that complemented the silvery drop earrings she wore.

Underneath her hair but braided into a small portion of her own hair at the nape of her neck lay the barely visible small cord of Donaldson tartan from her hand-fasting ceremony. On each tiny wrist she wore matching three-inch-wide hammered silver bracelet cuffs, which she had donned at the last minute knowing her mother would never approve.

As she walked, her clear three-inch heels gave her the appearance of being barefoot. The lovely bride carried a small bouquet of green roses with green-tinted baby's breath, which she held at her waist.

There was nothing plunging, off the shoulder, risqué, or revealing about her dress, though it hugged every curve of her figure. And it was there on the lowest part of her slender hips that the handiwork of Aunt Delores sat. The gift of clan tartan material had been fashioned into a low-slung, eight-inch-wide sash that wrapped around her to meet at a rosette gather on her left side. From the rosette fell the remaining six inches of material, which had been tightly pleated. This special item had also been added at the last minute, for Anne knew her mother would object to covering up any part of the wedding dress—especially given the adornment's location, just south of her waistline.

To Grant she looked like an angelic Celtic maiden, and he was unable to take his eyes off of her as the audience stood for the arrival of the bride. Anne made valiant attempts to acknowledge those in attendance as she walked by them but could hardly keep her eyes from returning Grant's gaze as he stood tall at the altar. She felt as though she were being presented to a handsome warrior prince who served the King of Kings.

As the last notes of the pipes played, she had finally reached the front, and her father took her hand to place it into Grant's big hand that was eagerly outstretched to receive her. Unexpectedly and untraditionally, she lowered her head and herself in a shallow and brief curtsy before him. Anne then took Grant's strong arm as he led her to the center of the altar area, facing the pastor.

As the final bagpipe notes hung in the air, Pastor Edwards spoke firmly, asking, "Who gives this woman to wed this man?" Anne could hear Ken Ledwell's voice coming from behind her, saying, "Her mother and I do." With that the pastor bade the attendees to be seated.

37

IF there existed a faint-less swoon, that would be what described Anne's state on seeing Grant again. Her knees felt like they would buckle just from his touch. Grant looked straight ahead at the pastor, for he was overwhelmed by the precious lovely standing next to him.

The pastor began methodically. "I have confirmed by virtue of a letter from Grant's pastor in Scotland that in December of last year, this couple announced their intent to marry before the church. Having received no objections there, I offer the same opportunity in this place. If there be anyone here today who has legal grounds to object to this marriage, speak now or forever hold your peace."

The few seconds of silence that intervened made Anne appreciate all that Pastor McGinty had done for them, and she wished he were here to see this. "Hearing none," Pastor Edwards intoned, "let us proceed."

The good reverend started by telling the congregation the couple's history for those who might not have known. He told the audience that Anne had accompanied her parents on a vacation through parts of the United Kingdom last September—her college graduation present. The two had first seen each other in Grant's church in Glasgow, where he sang a hymn he had written.

Moving on, Pastor Edwards told the crowd that the couple had had a brief first date the night before Anne left town with her parents. In ensuing months the couple got to know each other through letter writing. He told the crowd that in November, Grant's parents had invited Anne to return to Scotland to stay in their home over the Christmas holiday. It was during that visit that Anne and Grant confirmed their love for one another and Grant proposed marriage.

Pastor Edwards went on to explain the nuances of the hand-fasting ceremony and Anne's subsequent return to the United States, where wedding plans were made that brought her and Grant to the altar today—which also happened to be their shared birthday.

As they listened to Pastor Edwards recount their story in brief, both Anne and Grant mentally relived every detail he didn't speak of. Anne thought of Grant's tender moments of self-revelation and love, and Grant thought of how Anne could have won him without a word due to her sweet yet spirited nature. They both knew how much more of a story there was behind the short account that was given, and they treasured their story in their hearts.

Soon the pastor was asking Grant to face Anne for their vows. With Grant to repeat the pastor's words, the vows began:

"I, Grant Caelen Donaldson, take thee, Anne Elizabeth Ledwell, to be ma lawful wedded wife, ta have and ta hold from this day forward. I promise ta promote an defend spousal and family respect, ta love and cherish you for better or for worse, for richer or for poorer, in sickness and in health, till death us do part, according ta God's holy ordinance; and thereto I plight thee ma troth."

The pastor then turned to Anne:

"I, Anne Elizabeth Ledwell, take thee, Grant Caelen Donaldson, to be my lawful wedded husband, to have and to hold from this day forward. I promise to promote and defend spousal and family respect, to love and cherish you for better or for worse, for richer or for poorer, in sickness and in health, till death us do part, according to God's holy ordinance; and thereto I plight thee my troth."

Then Pastor Edwards asked the couple to repeat these words in unison after him:

"Entreat me not to leave you, or to return from following after you, for where you go, I will go, and where you are, there I will be also. Your people will be my people, and your God will be my God. May the Lord do with me and more if anything but death parts you from me."

Grant was asked if he had a ring to present to Anne as a symbol of his devotion, and he said yes. In an instant, he turned to Conor, who handed him the matching silver band to add to the silver diamond solitaire he had given her on Christmas Eve. As he began to place it on her finger, the pastor had him repeat these words: "With this ring I thee wed, with ma body I thee worship, an with all ma worldly goods I thee endow: In the name of the Father, an of the Son, an of the Holy Ghost. Amen."

Taking from Clara, her matron of honor, the simple silver band she had purchased for Grant, Anne placed it on his finger, repeating the same words. Only later would Grant find the tiny inscription on the inside of the ring–"There I will be also."

The pastor then said, "You have declared your consent before God and the Church. May the Lord in His goodness strengthen your consent and fill you both with His blessings. What therefore God has joined together, let no man put asunder. Amen."

He then said the words that Grant had been waiting to hear. "By the power vested in me by the state of New York, and on account of God's calling, I now pronounce you husband and wife. Grant—you may kiss your bride."

Exhibiting power in restraint, Grant held Anne's face with both hands and kissed her softly as the audience clapped.

The pastor then had the couple turn and face the crowd, and he announced, "Ladies and gentlemen, I present to you Mr. and Mrs. Grant Donaldson."

The crowd clapped again ... and Anne swore she even heard a yip. The pipes and strings had begun to play a light and airy recessional when Grant did the untraditional and unexpected by scooping her up into his arms and carrying Anne down the aisle!

Grant continued to carry Anne out of the chapel with her asking where he was taking her. Turning left past the doors of the chapel, he carried her into the open door of a side room that looked a bit like a small study or library. Without a word, he used his foot to shut the door behind them. Then he placed her gently against the wall where, standing in front of her, he put both of his hands against that same wall. She was like a small bird enclosed in a birdcage, and he had her right where he wanted her. He was breathing hard, but she didn't think it was because her hundred pounds was a weight to him.

"You must be the most beautiful bride ta ever walk the aisle," he began. "I was lost ta you in there—blind too, because I couldn't see anyone but you. Deaf, because I didn't want ta hear any voice but yours." He then began running one hand down from her neckline to cup her breast and then down to her waist, saying "An this beautiful frock ... it shows me everything on you that I want ta touch." With that he kissed her hard, and she wanted more.

Just then, Conor entered the room, obviously searching them out.

"There you are," he said. "The photographer is askin' the weddin' party ta return for pictures before we go ta the reception."

Grant slammed his hand against the wall, making a loud noise that startled Anne. Grant looked at Conor intently and said, "Would you look at this beauty that I haven't seen in five months, an tell me you can't buy me five minutes alone with her, man?"

Almost laughing, Conor held up both hands and backed away to the door, saying, "Right, big man. She is a beauty, an you got your five minutes—but that's it. That's as long as I can keep 'em at bay."

Alone again, it was now Anne's turn to speak.

"Let me tell you what I saw in there. I saw a strong fortress of a man, my Adonis ... and I want you with everything in me." This time she threw her arms around his neck while he wrapped his arms around her waist, and they kissed passionately again.

Finally, they sensed that their time was probably up. As they collected themselves to reenter the chapel, Anne grabbed

Grant's hand and coyly inquired, "Is it true that Scottish men don't wear anything under their kilts?"

Grant grinned at her and said, "I believe I'll let you think on that for a wee bit longer, lass."

38

AFTER posing for pictures, the family and wedding party moved to the room where the lunch reception was being held. Grant and Anne were the last to enter the room, and it erupted in applause. Off in the corner, the Celtic music troupe had regrouped and was starting to play again for the crowd that was in various stages of collecting food from the buffet tables. The last thing on Anne's mind was food, but she figured she must eat while she could.

She and Grant spotted the larger round table in the front and center of the room reserved for the Donaldson and Ledwell families. They took this opportunity to set things down on the table—Grant removing the plaid and brooch from his shoulder and loosening his tie, while Anne unhooked her tartan sash and set it on the table. However, she took her bouquet and placed it right in front of Gena, saying, "Let's just pretend I threw it and that you caught it!"

Now more comfortable, they started mingling with the attendees. They finally made their way to the buffet, where everyone insisted that they cut in line. Grant apparently was hungry because he took them up on that right away! As they carried their plates back to the table, they passed the beautiful wedding cake that Grant was seeing for the first time. It was a three-tiered white cake with two frosting flowers on top—a purple thistle and a red rose. Anne winked at him and said, "Chocolate inside."

Returning to sit down, they found that many of the family members were settling in too. Anne noticed that Mr. Donaldson and her father were sitting next to each other and already engaged in discussion. The mothers were on the other sides of their husbands, so they were talking with their daughters. It was such a joy to see the two families together—for what Grant and Anne assumed might be one of the few times they would be together. Before they took their first bites of food, Grant turned to face Anne and took her hands in his and began to pray quietly so that only Anne could hear. With his amen, he kissed her on the forehead and turned to his plate to dig in.

The music was lovely, the food was great, and the company was best of all. But the surprising entertainment was just getting started. It seemed that Grant and his band mates had a plan after eating, and it involved cutting in on the orchestra.

Grant excused himself from the table after Ian approached him to whisper something. Before Anne knew it, the men had given the wedding musicians a "break" and were borrowing their instruments. With Andrew at the piano and Grant, Conor, and Ian having taken their places in front, the crowd hushed as the piano played a simple intro.

Anne was so happy that her friends and family would actually get to hear what she had told them about. The strong male voices in harmony rose out in a beautiful song about their homeland. The song also involved each one singing a short solo part, and it really showed off their individual talents. The group was a big hit, and Anne was so proud of them.

After the song, they returned the stage to the regular band, but not without vowing to get George Donaldson up to sing another number later. The old man waved them off, but Grant assured Anne that he'd get his dad up there to sing yet.

Not to be outdone, Anne rose from her chair, kissed Grant on his bald head, and walked to the front of the room. She had done a little behind-the-scenes preparation with the musicians during the previous weeks, and one of them handed her a microphone. The crowd hushed again. Grant turned his chair to face her directly and listen intently.

She began by saying, "I first want to say that it is Grant who is, and will always be, the real musical talent in the family, but I thought I'd sing to him for a change. I wrote this song about a month ago when I was missing him so much. I love you, Grant." With that, a single violin drew out a slow, sweet tune, and Anne began to sing in her beautiful middle soprano voice:

You called to me from across the deep. I came to you in a faith-born leap.

I did not know whither you might be. Your song led me there, where I could see.

Across the room in a crowded space, there I beheld your winsome face.

For just a moment all time stood still; love finds a way with its strong will.

Now I am yours, and you are mine; we'll walk together to the edge of time . . . to the edge of time.

The crowd went wild with applause, and Grant stood up clapping. He then made his way to Anne's side and put his arm around her and took the microphone to say, "Can you believe it—she's lovely an she can sing too?"

In response, George Donaldson shouted out from the head table, "Aye, but can she cook?"

That brought the whole house down, and Anne was certain she'd never seen her father laugh so hard in her life. Over all the din and laughter, Grant responded to his father by slowly looking at Anne from head to toe and then stating, "Dad . . . I don't care," which just made the crowd roar even more. With that, Grant said, "I think we'll go cut the cake so you can all 'ave some!"

On the way to the cake table, Grant put his arm around Anne's waist and whispered to her, "That was amazin'–you cannot keep that voice hidden away, Anne. You must promise me you'll sing it again when we get home for our celebration at the church . . . and again at Mac's."

Anne appeased him with an okay, but she was hoping he'd not insist on it when they did get back to Scotland. Besides, she didn't even know there'd be a celebration at the church upon their return.

The couple fed each other cake as the photographer snapped more pictures. While they were posing for a final shot, Andrew stood on his chair at his table and had everyone singing happy birthday to the couple!

In the process of returning to their table while thanking people along the way, Grant noticed for the first time a large table with gifts on it. He looked at Anne and asked, "Are those for us?"

"Oh yes," Anne responded. "But my parents will have to ship them to us after we tell them where to send them."

They were interrupted when Conor cut in to tell Grant that he was going to get the boys to grab Mr. Donaldson and get him up to the front. Anne returned to her seat, stopping by to thank and hug both mothers and sisters again. Her father stood up and gave her a big hug, whispering in her ear, "I've always thought you had a beautiful voice after all those years of hearing it during church. That was really something, sweetie. And your young man also has great talent."

Anne smiled and said, "Thank you, Daddy—for everything."

Just then, three Scottish lads were grabbing Mr. Donaldson by the arms and hauling him to the front, while Grant leaned over to whisper to Anne, "You've heard this song before, so at the last verse, jes gather up our things an be ready ta make an escape with me." Her heart started racing at the thought of finally being alone with Grant on their honeymoon!

The men were up front and began to sing a capella in a stunning harmony that had the crowd on the edges of their seats. This number sounded even more Gaelic, even using many words from the ancient language. It was about their homeland, history, and national pride. Halfway through the song, Anne noticed there were even some tears shed by a few in the room. A crescendo grew as the singers came to the last verse, which is when Grant turned to shake hands with his father, who was standing next to him—singing out loud and proud.

Anne took that as a cue. She threw Grant's plaid over her shoulders and gathered up their things from the table. Grant left the group and beckoned to her to come to his side while the powerful song was coming to conclusion and the men were raising their hands to the sky. The couple waved to the attendees and dashed out to the foyer and through the front doors of the church to a waiting car and driver that Anne's father had engaged to take them to the hotel.

Anne was relieved to see their small overnight bags tucked away in the front seat as they slid into the backseat and drove away. Conor and Clara had done an excellent job of tending to the couple behind the scenes all day. And what a day it had been! Now they could fall into each other's arms and would soon enjoy the full measure of their love for one another.

39

WITH Grant following behind her carrying their two small bags, Anne opened the door to their lovely tenth-floor hotel room. The small alcove entryway of the room was dimly lit when they walked in. Grant immediately dropped the bags by the door and pulled Anne close to kiss her, locking the deadbolt with one hand as he did so.

One kiss led to another, and both were breathing harder with each kiss. With one hand searching desperately for the zipper of Anne's dress, Grant was getting nowhere, so Anne put a halt to the kissing by putting her index finger to his mouth.

"Now listen carefully," she said. "I am going to turn around so you can unzip this wedding dress. It starts at the top and ends at my low back. I want you to do it slowly, not because I'm worried about the dress, but because I don't want you to miss anything as you do this. Understood?"

Grant nodded his understanding, and she turned around.

He located the hidden zipper and began to slowly draw it down—passing her slender back, where he noticed she was not wearing a bra. Then he passed a small tan birthmark on the way down. Anne felt the dress peeling off her front, so she held onto it with her arms and hands.

As Grant reached the very end of the zipper, he realized that she was not wearing anything under this dress, so he slowly turned her around to face him. As he did, she released the dress, which fell to her feet. His eyes feasted on her nakedness as she stood vulnerable before him. For just a second he closed his eyes, as though it was too much to take in. Then he picked her up and carried her to the bed, while she slipped off her shoes and let them drop on the floor along the way.

Grant had still not said a word since they entered the room. But setting her gently on the bed, he whispered to her, "Pearhaps I am overdressed for this occasion," and began to remove his jacket, tie, shoes, socks, belt, and shirt. Anne was literally shaking, and she couldn't seem to control it. The combination of her love for him, the excitement of his undressing before her, and a dash of new-bride anxiety was causing her to quake.

Finally, as he began to unwrap his kilt, she had the additional thrill of having her earlier question answered. As it dropped to the floor, he moved into position over her body, carefully holding his weight with his strong arms so as not to apply too much pressure to her small frame.

For the first time she knew what it felt like to be skin-to-skin with her lover, and the delight was beyond intense. Even as he repeatedly kissed her, he could feel her shaking beneath him. He stopped only for a moment to assure her that he would be careful but also to remind her that this was what he'd been waiting for. As he entered her body for the first time, she felt a brief sting, which then melted into pure bliss. He rocked her slowly in his arms, and the two climaxed simultaneously in their first union.

It took several minutes for the waves of shuddering to pass—for both of them were in awe of the wedding gift they had just opened together. As their heavy breathing subsided, he told her he loved her and how satisfying she was to him. They rested together for several minutes as Anne caressed and explored his face, neck, and chest with her hands. Then she quietly asked him, "Can we do that again?"

He chuckled, which she felt both inside and outside of her body. He responded by informing her, "You'll need ta give me some recovery time, lass."

She didn't say anything, allowing another minute or so to pass, but she had yet another question. "How much recovery time is required?" she eagerly asked.

Grant smiled broadly on account of her continued innocence and raised himself up to kiss her again, saying, "Let's jes say you shouldn't plan ta be leavin' this bed anytime soon."

40

THEIR forty-eight hours together was full of tenderness, abandon, trust, and cherishment. Tucked away in their room, they had started to exercise their vows: "With my body, I thee worship."

As they now shut the door to their tenth-floor haven to depart on Monday, Grant stopped once more to lean down to kiss Anne, saying, "I will never forget the bond we have forged in these few days together."

Anne flashed a big smile and asked, "Was that what we were doing in there?"

Oh, how he loved his spirited wife—and how much he loved that her desires were only for him . . . forever.

When they were dropped off by cab at the apartment building, Ben was waiting on the sidewalk to meet the newlyweds. Anne introduced Grant to Ben, and the two shook hands heartily. Ben leaned over with his hand covering half his mouth, but not even trying to keep a secret from Anne, as he spoke to Grant. "I hope you know you done picked the most lovely lady in this here city—so congratulations."

Grant smiled and said, "I do know, even without seein' any other ladies in this city—thank you!"

Before the couple caught the elevator up to the apartment, Anne gave Ben a big hug—whispering in his ear, "I'm going to miss you, Big Ben."

Anne's parents were expecting them and had heard Ben announce them on the intercom to their apartment. The front door was opening as the newlyweds reached it. Ken and Ruth were thrilled to see the couple and had them put their bags in Anne's bedroom. This was the first time Grant had seen her white bedspread, where she told him she had read his letters over and over, and the desk from which she had written to him.

Within minutes Ruth was informing them that there was lunch on the table for them, so they should eat, as they'd need to repack their separate things together and make decisions about what they could take with them on the plane.

The four had a great lunch together—reliving the wedding and talking about the wonderful dinner the families and friends had on Sunday night. It was quite obvious from the discussion that Grant's and Anne's fathers had really hit it off.

Grant seemed a bit more nervous around her parents and in their home than Anne had expected, but she chalked it up to the speed at which the whole relationship had progressed. As that thought entered her head, she almost laughed out loud, considering how it all seemed to drag on forever in her recollection. She had to remember that from the perspective of family members, she and Grant had met on one day, gotten engaged on another day, gotten acquainted for three additional days, and then married on day six!

The two then spent the rest of the afternoon opening gifts, keeping a list for follow-up thank-you notes, and trying to figure out what they needed to pack for immediate use when they got home. It was tricky, but by 4:30 p.m. they had locked the last suitcase and were ready to head to Newark airport with her parents. Ken had rented a car for the weekend and a few more days, so there'd be one last opportunity to eat out (Ruth was happy) and talk about how they would keep in touch (Ken was happy).

After stopping for dinner along the way, they arrived at the airport, and it was time to say good-bye. Ken Ledwell was never one for long good-byes at the gate, so Anne knew this was going to be a quick procedure for him. Ruth hugged them both and started to tear up, but when Ken hugged Grant for the first time and called him "son," Anne started crying. She had always been a daddy's girl, so this was gut-wrenching for her. She had hardly been able to admit to him that there was another man in her life when she first met Grant, but now she had to say good-bye to the man who had nurtured and cherished her for the first twenty-three years of her life. She held onto her father for several minutes, while Grant thanked his in-laws for all they had done for them.

Anne thanked her parents for her graduation present again, reminding them that it was a gift that had changed the course of her life forever. Then Ken took her hand, and again placed it into Grant's hand, saying, "God bless you both. Be sure to write."

As they began to part ways, Grant assured her parents that Anne would be well cared for. And having regained her composure, Anne chimed in with her imitation brogue, "They 'ave ta take good care of me, for I am Clan Donaldson naw!"

By the time Anne and Grant had stationed themselves at their gate to await the boarding call, they were emotionally spent. Grant just put his arm around her, and she rested her head on his shoulder. They were quiet for several minutes—both processing all that had taken place in the last three days.

It was Grant who broke the silence first. Kissing her forehead, he observed, "I thought I knew what you were givin' up when you conceded ta live in Scotland. I didn't know the half of it, Anne. You have a great family, an this is a great land with so much bounty an opportunity. I want you ta know I don't take it for granted what you give up to be with me."

She looked up from his shoulder and said, "It's not a subtraction in my life, and I would never consider marrying you as something to count as loss. I love you, Grant, and our lives will be better together than they ever could have been individually. We are a team."

The contented lovers slept in each other's arms during the overnight flight. When Anne wasn't asleep, she enjoyed watching Grant sleep. She studied him intently every chance she got. And each time she did, she'd end up thanking God for her beloved protector and provider. That seam they had stitched together in December was now a seamless fusion of their hearts. And as the final flight was preparing to land, the couple held hands as they touched down in Scotland again. This time, it was as husband and wife, starting a new life together with all its hopes and dreams.

41

FROM the airport where Grant had left his car, they were met with a beautiful sunny and mild temperature afternoon. Though she didn't know it now, Anne would soon come to love the long spring and summer daylight hours at this latitude, though the more prevalent rain would take some getting used to. As they drove along the way, things started to look more familiar to her—especially when they passed the church. Though she knew the apartment wasn't much to work with, she nonetheless looked forward to being "home."

As Grant pulled into the driveway, Anne noticed a sweet handmade sign on the front porch that said, "Welcome home." Grant didn't drive to the rear of the house, but instead parked in front and turned off the car. He then turned to Anne and put his hand on hers.

She thought she saw him swallow hard before he began.

"Anne, I didn't want ta bring it up during these last days, but you need ta know naw that Mrs. McBride took ill in March. She got so bad that I had ta carry her from her couch ta ma car ta the infirmary one night. It was pneumonia; an she was in a bad way. I spent the week visitin' and sittin' with her in hospital each night after ma work, but she jes worsened. She slipped away on a Sunday night.

"But I had time with her, an she knew she was loved. It wasn't until April that a solicitor contacted me ta tell me she had reverted this house ta me on her second day in hospital. So, I suppose in a way, she left us a weddin' present. This is naw our home, Anne, though I'm sorry ta have ta tell you the sad news that comes with it."

Anne had tears growing heavier on her eyelids as Grant told the story, and now they spilled over the edges and onto his hand that held hers. He felt helpless to spare her the bittersweet news.

Through her tears, Anne said, "Grant—she did this because you looked after her. And God has honored you for having cared for this widow, which pleases Him."

He squeezed her hand and asked, "Are you ready to go inside?"

She was very ready.

As they got out of the car, they left their things in the trunk to return for them later. Walking up to the small front porch, Grant told her the sign was Gena's handiwork. However, he explained that Gwen, his father, his mother, his brother-in-law, and friends had also done some work over the last six weeks to put the place into better shape for her arrival. As he unlocked the door, he picked her up to carry her across the threshold of their home. He then kissed her before putting her down in her living room.

She hadn't seen much of the place outside of the kitchen and upstairs apartment in the back of the house, so she wasn't aware of all the work that had gone into improvements. As he showed her around the house, Grant pointed out the fresh paint, repairs, the fireplace he'd cleaned himself, the windows Gwen had washed, the pillows on the couch that his mother had made, and a beautiful old grandfather clock by the door that his father had found, refurbished, and donated to the cause, as well as the new kitchen table and chairs his mates had found secondhand and refinished. Anne was so happy, for next to Grant, home was so very important to her. She loved how cozy and simple it was.

Grant continued his tour but was now beginning to promise to paint the exterior and more. She just stopped him and kissed him, telling him not to rush—they had a lifetime together, remember? He agreed but eagerly pulled on her arm to bring her to see their bedroom. He was beaming with pride to show her all the work that had gone into this little sanctuary. The women in the family had definitely been working overtime to create a lovely bedspread and matching curtains. And they'd even placed a pretty milk-glass vase containing a bouquet of flowers on the dresser for their homecoming.

Anne told him it was all beautiful and that she'd simply add her touch to make the home a refuge and solace for him. He grabbed her by the waist and started kissing her while inching her toward the bed—telling her that she was his refuge, and that he "could use a little solace" at that moment.

42

THE remaining days of the week were days off for Grant before he needed to return to the shop, so the newlyweds made the most of each one. They even had the other Mr. and Mrs. Donaldson come over for a dinner that Anne struggled to make, for she still had much to learn in that category. Pastor McGinty and his wife stopped by their home for tea, and the four of them did a prayer walk around the property boundary and the house. It was an intimate time together as the four sought God's blessing and protection over the home. It also gave the two couples time to discuss the small marriage celebration and reception that the church family wanted to have for Grant and Anne about ten days hence.

Grant continued his work on transforming his old boarding room upstairs above the kitchen into his studio, to be able to practice and write songs. And Anne had written her first letter to her parents to tell them the news of their home and provide them with information about how and where to send along the remaining wedding gifts. Of course, they spent much time in each other's arms upon their marriage bed, just as Grant had longed for on the lonely nights before they were married.

On Saturday night, the band would play again at Mac's, and Anne was excited about that. It was really the only form of night on the town they could afford. Affordable because Mac provided a free meal and one drink to Anne and each of the band members, on the house. Though Mac gave the singing group a small payment for their services, once they divided it up, it just covered a bit of petrol in the car for a week . . . if they didn't drive much.

But this night something presented itself that Anne wasn't expecting. It wasn't that things seemed different. In fact, Mac was even friendlier and more doting after Anne, and the band members were like brothers to her now. As she settled into a small table near the side of the stage where the lights were dimmer, she looked forward to hearing many of the songs she'd tried to commit to memory—at least the ones in English. She enjoyed them all over again, as well as some new songs—most of them written by Grant, who seemed to be the poet among them all. Given his expressions in letter writing, she wasn't surprised.

But as the performance was coming close to the last few numbers, Grant sang a solo that he had written. It was a song that most assuredly was in English, for Anne understood every word as it advanced a story of a young man who had lost his family to the cruelty of violent war waged by the English in their efforts to disperse the clans. With each verse, the words grew harsher, and Grant expressed them by almost spitting out the words as he spoke of the famine, torture, hatred, and murder.

Anne was unable to move a muscle during this gripping song, but it was also tearing her apart inside. Though she was American by birth and culture, she couldn't help but be confronted by the bloodguilt of her English ancestors portrayed in Grant's song. Tears of conviction, self-consciousness, and even fear were running down her cheeks as Grant completed the final verse, which projected anger, resentment, and an ongoing resistance to forgiving those who had carried out these deeds against the Scottish people.

The moment the song ended, and the crowd was clapping in what all of a sudden looked like an angry mob, Anne moved quickly from her chair, past the bar, and down the hallway to a lavatory in the back of the pub. Passing a drunken couple who were holding each other up by kissing, she ran into the small, dank bathroom and buried her face in her hands as she cried. Her mind raced back over the words and Grant's stern face as he sang them. Did he feel these words and this way? Was she to blame for the deeds of her ancestors who betrayed and murdered his people by the tens of thousands at a time? How could he reconcile this? How could she?

Grant had noticed Anne's sudden departure from her now empty table by the side of the stage but didn't see her tears or make any connection around her disappearance. However, he did wish she'd been there for their last song, about the love of a young Welsh couple separated by parental disapproval.

As the band took their bows and exited off the back of the stage, Grant instead climbed down the few steps in front to hustle through the crowd to find Anne. Some fans tried to get him to stop and talk, but he excused himself politely and kept moving toward the back hallway to check on her. As he did, Anne emerged from the hallway entrance, where they almost collided.

Relieved to see her, he put his arms around her and started to say something when he noticed her red-rimmed eyelids and her arms by her sides—not typical of the girl who always reciprocated his hugs.

"I don't understand, Anne . . . are you not well?" he inquired of her. She looked up at him and asked him to take her away from there—home, yes, that's where she wanted to go.

Grant put his arm around her shoulder and guided her through the crowds to the backstage area. He had her wait outside the room where his mates were relaxing after the show, rather than force her to make small talk. Gathering his guitar and congratulating them on a great show, he made his excuses to depart immediately. The boys gave him a hard time about his new "marital duties" keeping him from their club antics, but he waved them off and returned to take Anne to the car.

With the car doors closed, he asked her if she was ready to tell him what was bothering her.

The tears started to flow again, making it hard for her to speak. She sniffled through with, "Grant, that song you sang about the English . . . do you—do others around here still feel that way about my ancestors? Am I to be an anathema to the very people I will make my home with?"

Grant was surprised by her questions and her reaction. He took a deep breath for he sensed that this would take some time to explain to one with a history of just a few days in his motherland.

"Anne, first I want ta say that I am pearsonally encouraged that this ballad has brought on such strong emotion. That's ma music's goal, but it ceartainly wasn't ma goal ta hurt you in any way.

"I want you ta put the song in context as we talk about this, lass. These are the words of a lad from the 1700s—not ma words or thoughts today. They're words from a day gone by—an how they must have felt then. Do you understand that?"

Anne nodded her head up and down, allowing him to go on.

"Havin' said that, I don't want ta tell you there are no residual anti-Anglo feelings in this country, Anne. Though most of us would be happy with home rule, there are some very independence-minded politicians here, though their influence is on the wane. An most of those are in the minority, so you can't go about livin' your life here carryin' such thoughts about the Scots. Ma people will hear you as an American, an while there be some who carry negative feelin' toward those, it's also a minority.

"So, please don't take this song into the present, lass. It's meant ta reflect the past. Does it raise some nationalism in us when we replay our history as Scots? Yes, I cannot deny that, but you are not a target. I will not let you be, for I have vowed ta promote an defend spousal an family respect. You are mine, an I am yours. Same team, right?"

As he lifted her chin to check her mood, she fell into his arms.

43

THE long days of summer in Scotland gave way to the colors of fall early that September. Though Anne missed her family back in the United States, she kept in touch by letter and the very occasional phone call. It was later in the month when she received word that she was an auntie again—this time to Clara's baby boy, named Joshua. That news came from her parents, who offered to fly her and Grant to New York for Christmas to gather with Victoria and Clara and her growing family. Grant was thrilled at the prospect of seeing more of New York City.

While she loved her family very much, Anne's heart had quickly started to put down roots in her new home of Scotland. Grant took every opportunity he had to show her his beloved country, and he thought she might even be gaining "a wee bit of an accent." Anne eagerly pursued books on Scottish history and could spend hours roaming through the free museums and galleries. Similarly, she had gotten to know some of her neighbors and, of course, had made friends at church. One of the many things she had thrown herself into was learning more about cooking from her mother-in-law, and Grant conceded that she was "making progress" on that front.

Grant was dutiful about his job at the shop but still managed to find time to write lyrics and music. For Christmas that year, Anne presented Grant with a Scottish whistle, which he took to learning immediately. But nothing occupied his heart more than Anne. He knew before they were married that she was selfless, but he was continually amazed at her willingness to put others first—especially him.

Grant and Anne had much to learn from and about each other, which they did for decades to come. It was how they built upon their marriage. They were builders, not the types to tear things or others down. They built a life together; they built into each other; they built a family; they even built onto the small house. They built wealth; they built friendships; they built Grant's musical career; they built into their church and into the Kingdom of God on Earth.

EPILOGUE

GRANT and Anne Donaldson still reside in Glasgow, where they work and play in the fields of the Lord.

Anne turned out to be quite the wealth manager, turning profits on multiple cottage industries over the years—even obtaining a few patents. She also did some importing and exporting, and for a time she worked at the university. And of course, her investments have done well—including those original stocks she gave Grant at their first Christmas together.

Saving up funds early in their marriage, she was able to get Grant and the band to London for their first recording session, which paved the way for success at home and abroad. She even located and engaged their first agent, having often handled the business end of the music in the early days. She restricts her own singing, however, to the church choir these days, though the congregation loves it when she and Grant sing duets once or twice a year.

Owing to Anne's vision and his great talent, Grant's dream became a reality when his music eventually became his work.

He has written numerous songs, which the group performed on multination tours, but has also published solo recordings. He even published a book of poetry a few years ago. He is one of Glasgow's favored sons, and the city authorities officially named him their resident troubadour and laureate. He is also the recipient of several music industry accolades, but through it all he has always remained himself—loving his family, giving back to his hometown, caring for friends, serving as a deacon in the church, and even occasionally performing at Mac's—now under new management.

Anne and Grant have not been without heartaches, the worst being the delivery of a stillborn baby boy whom they buried after naming him Paul Shuard Donaldson. It brought both physical and emotional pain to Anne, and Grant suffered in the loss of another son. However, two years later they took great joy in the birth of Eden Ellen Donaldson. Their daughter became a beautiful woman with thick chestnut-red hair, a peaches-and-cream complexion, and a voice like an angel. That voice was a perfect fit with her instrument of choice—the harp. She and her father occasionally perform together, and Eden has collaborated on several of his recordings.

Grant and Anne still love intensely, and life is like a song.

CPSIA information can be obtained
at www.ICGtesting.com
Printed in the USA
LVOW12s0405040516
486614LV00001B/25/P